GIRLS ARE EQUAL TOO

GIRLS ARE EQUAL TOO

How To Survive For Teenage Girls

Dale Carlson
Hannah Carlson, M.Ed., C.R.C.
Illustrations By Carol Nicklaus

BICK PUBLISHING HOUSE   1998   MADISON, CT

First published by Atheneum in hardcover in eight printings 1973 -1980
Aladdin Paperback 1973
Published simultaneously in Canada by McClelland & Stewart, Ltd.
Manufactured in the United States of America

SECOND EDITION
Edited by Director Editorial Ann Maurer
Senior Editor Sharyn Skeeter
Book Design by Jennifer A. Payne
Cover Design by Greg Sammons

Library of Congress Cataloging-in-Publication Data

Carlson, Dale Bick.
    Girls are equal too : how to survive : for teenage girls / Dale Carlson and Hannah Carlson : illustrations by Carol Nicklaus. --2nd ed.
        p.   cm.
    "ALA notable book"--Cover.
    Includes bibliographical references and index.
    ISBN 1-884158-18-8
    1. Feminism--Juvenile literature. 2. Girls--Juvenile literature. [1. Women's rights. 2. Women--History.} I. Carlson, Hannah. II. Nicklaus, Carol. III. Title.
HQ1154.C335 1998
305.42--dc21   97-31718
                                                                    CIP
                                                                    AC

**Completely Rewritten
And Updated For The Next Millennium**

IN
DEDICATION

To all the young people everywhere who have answered, sometimes painfully, always honestly, our questions about their lives and feelings for so many years. And to their parents, teachers, and the librarians who helped to organize groups for our dialogues.

To Toni Mendez, agent, mentor, and friend for her decades of love and faith. To Ann Maurer, editor, for her skill, tact, and constant support. To Jean Karl of Atheneum, who first believed in, guided, and published this book, great gratitude.

To our next generation: Sam, Chaney, Malcolm — and Shannon. May you have the strength and clarity to understand that behavior is catching.

With our love.

BOOKS BY DALE CARLSON

FICTION:
The Mountain Of Truth
The Human Apes
Triple Boy
Baby Needs Shoes
Call Me Amanda
Charlie The Hero
The Plant People

NONFICTION:
Manners That Matter
Wildlife Care For Birds And Mammals

with HANNAH CARLSON

NONFICTION:
Living With Disabilities
Basic Manuals For Friends Of The Disabled
    6 Volume Series
Where's Your Head?: Psychology For Teenagers

CONTENTS

Introduction
THE PUT-DOWN

Section One
THE WAY IT IS

Growing Up A Girl	3
Girls In School	11
Girls And Boys	23
Women In College	33
Women At Work	43
Women And The Arts	53
Women's Image In Advertising & *What They Do To You At The Mall*	61
There's Something Wrong With Your Rights	69
The Beautiful Imbecile	83
The Happy Housewife	93

Section Two
HOW WE GOT THIS WAY

Adam And Eve   105

The Bound Foot   113

The Empty Mind   123

The Feminist Struggle   133

Back To The Cave   145

The Beginning Of Success   157

Section Three
WHAT YOU CAN DO ABOUT IT

Think Straight   167

What About Boys?   179

What About Work?   187

What About Marriage?   199

The Fight For Your Own Survival   213

INDEX

SUGGESTED READING and
SELECTED BIBLIOGRAPHY

Introduction:
The Put-Down

L ike every other girl, you have a lot to learn. And some of the lessons aren't easy. The first, and most basic lesson, is learning to be stupid. You may already have discovered this.

Learning to be stupid is hard. It takes years of work on your part, and an exhausting amount of effort on the part of society. All of it intended to make sure that when you grow up, you will know practically nothing. Or at least, a lot less than boys.

Never mind that you get good marks in arithmetic (girls do get consistently better marks in school than boys). You will still not be allowed to admit that you can balance a check-book or do a spreadsheet.

Never mind that you can play a computer better than a rock musician a keyboard. You will still need to suggest you hardly know how to turn a monitor on.

Never mind that you know how to change a tire on a pickup truck (with a good jack, it takes less physical effort to change a tire than to scrub a floor). You will not be allowed to grasp anything so mechanical.

Never mind that you know how to read (which you have probably been doing since you were six). You will still not be allowed to understand the contents of books, magazines, or the instructions that come with the VCR.

Never mind that you will probably have spent twelve, sixteen, or more years in school (depending on how long it takes you to learn not to learn). When you apply for a job and want equal pay, interesting challenges, a position that leads to top management, someone will look at you as if you were crazy or joking or both.

As I said, it takes years to learn that lesson in stupidity.

Which brings us to the second difficult task: learning to be inferior. It is not enough to know less than boys, you must be less.

Never mind that your intelligence is the same, your ability to work is the same (plus you can have a baby if you want to). You will not be allowed even to hint at your equality, much less any superiority.

Never mind that girls have greater endurance (we sustain activity, cold, fatigue, longer; we even live longer). You are still the weaker sex.

Never mind that you were born with greater verbal, perceptual, and analytical skills than boys (which means that if girls were brought up the same as boys, girls would be in a better position to cope with the world than boys are). You are still not fit to make decisions or be a leader.

Never mind that it doesn't make sense to be inferior. Just hang your head and stand there. Above all, do this quietly and politely. You may have the voice and disposition of a chain-saw, but display these only if you wish to be thrown into the jaws of an alligator.

The third lesson girls have to learn is how to be passive. From the beginning of their lives, boys are brought up to go out and do something and reap the rewards. What girls are brought up to do is stand around and watch, or help the boys, or at least reap a lot less.

You're good at sports and you'd like to be on a team? You may get a medal, but you probably won't get a boy. Be a cheerleader, and let the boys do the winning. Then getting a boy is easy.

You have an aptitude for biology? Fine, but be a pediatrician. That way, you won't compete too much with the brain surgeons, and you'll have lots of chances to clap for the male medical establishment. (The same rule holds for any field. Interested in law or government? Marry the President of the United States. Good at writing or art? Don't do it, teach it.

Have a bent for science? Avoid the creative aspects of research and be a lab technician.)

While it's perfectly true that you have excellent legs for standing or running on and an able mind to think with, avoid using them at all costs. Use only the hands, to clap with. And when you get tired of clapping for your boyfriend or eventually your husband, don't worry. You can always have sons and clap for them. (Not your daughters, however. Remember, they, too, have to learn to be stupid, inferior, and passive.)

Passivity, of course, leads neatly into the fourth necessity for a girl: dependence. A really good girl is not just passive, she takes it one step farther. She leans a little. Girls are not naturally more nervous or fearful than boys. They're just told they are. They're brought up that way.

You may be able to cope with your homework, teach your parents how to use a computer, form a political opinion, get and hold a job. But you should not do these things without pretending your able competence is just really good guesswork. It makes people happy to think of you as a helpless child.

It's even better, of course, if you bungle your work and can't begin to form an opinion of your own. You'll lose everybody's respect and your self-respect along with it. But you'll find everybody thinks you're as adorable as a pet poodle.

And that brings us to an extremely important matter: being adorable. A truly feminine girl has to be beautiful at all times.

You're not all that frantically interested in clothes and makeup, dieting and working out, developing big breasts on a long, thin body topped by highlighted or straightened hair? Get interested. Hang by your thumbs till you're tall, diet till you're half dead from anorexia and bulimia, try every kind of makeup, three hairdos, low heels, high heels, miniskirts, tight pants, loose shirts, tight sweaters, tattoos, and you still don't look like the beach girls on a TV sitcom? Try again. Go on trying until you die trying. Men don't have to be beautiful, but you do! Of course, if getting gorgeous enough to be popular also gets you early sexual harassment (this is happening as young as eight, nine, ten years old in school halls these days), abused or raped at home or in the streets, remember to go on acting innocent as the morning dew on a rose. Whatever happens to them, girls are supposed to be sweet, innocent, and ladylike at all times.

Girls are also not supposed to know they feel the same strong desires as boys, for success, for rebellion, even for sex. So naturally they are unprepared for winning, for rage, for the accidents of unwanted pregnancy, AIDS, STD's (sexually transmitted diseases), and other disasters.

Are you remembering your lessons?

- Even if I win, I lose? (This is related to your general understanding of your own stupidity.)

- Even if I could pick him up and throw him across the gym, he's stronger.

- Even if I'm into advanced calculus or get straight A's, and he's till struggling with last year's spelling test — he's smarter.

- Even if I have to walk on my knees to date him, remember, he's taller.

- Even if everybody wants me for class president, I'll bribe them not to vote for me against a boy. You're supposed to serve men, not lead them. Avoid all success like the plague!

Add anything you like to this list. And understand, you have to please not only boys, but also parents, teachers, and the rest of society.

- Even if you have a strong character, crumple.

- Even if you're weird, act straight.

- Of course, if you're gay, act straight.

- If you're a homegirl, behave yourself and act like a schoolgirl.

- If you're African American, Hispanic American, Asian American, Native American, act both black or brown or copper or yellow or freckled *and* white, so you can get a job.

- If you have weird legs and a crooked nose and a flat chest, fix yourself with plastic surgery. Remember, your value is your body parts.

- If you belong to the ten percent of the population who have physical, observable disabilities (everyone has hidden disabilities), make even more sure, if you are a girl, that you remain cheerful, passive, and compliant at all times.

- And if ever you should happen to feel like removing someone else's face, at least have a stupid, sweet, docile, compliant, nice, and polite expression on your own.

All of this will, of course, frustrate you terribly. And you won't EVER get used to it. But somebody will be there to pay the bills when you gnash your teeth to the nerves, get terrible stomach cramps, are knocked flat with tension headaches, or need psychiatric help. Somebody else will have to pay the bills — you'll never be allowed to be successful enough to pay them all yourself.

Speaking of FRUSTRATION — well, we've hardly begun. Besides being expected to play with plastic kitchens while boys can explore the real world of fields and city streets, and having to keep your pink skirt or cropped shorts and skimpy T-shirt clean while boys can wear anything they want and get it dirty, and being allowed to jump rope while boys run and climb and really develop their bodies — besides all that, you're supposed to be NICE about it.

If a boy punched you in the stomach, did anybody approve of you if you punched him back? Of course not. Nice girls are gentle.

If a brother or sister took your toys or borrowed your possessions without asking, did people approve if you made a loud noise about it? Of course not. Nice girls are kind, giving, and above all QUIET.

And how about the times you came home late for supper, left your room in a mess, forgot to do your homework, got dirty, had a fight, disobeyed someone's orders, yelled for attention or spat spitballs in a classroom? Hah! Boys will be boys, but girls must be obedient, clean, and quiet at all times.

Of course, if you insisted on climbing trees, playing baseball, having adventures, and wearing an old pair of pants every day, if you hit or yelled back when you were hit or called bad names, sexually harassed or worse, offered drugs, guns, gang violence, a little criminal participation, you were called a tomboy. Maybe, up to a point, everybody even thought you were cute, fighting back. But that foolishness is supposed to straighten out when you finally realize, sometimes as early as seven or eight, but certainly by your midteens, your true function in life. You may be traumatized by anorexia, date rape, a pregnant thirteen-year-old sister, the news that your best friend tested HIV-positive, parents and teachers neglecting your need for competence and work, for confidence and freedom to bloom and grow, but you will still not be allowed to forget your primary function.

Your true function in life — have you figured out what that is yet? Have you properly understood what the whole put-down is really leading up to? The bringing up (or, rather, bringing down) of most girls qualifies them to become, not mature intelligent adults with the right to call their souls and dreams their own, but only part of that vast, domestic army that nurtures, supports, takes care of everybody else. The function is called the housewife, the mother, or the maid. In short, not a person, only a female.

The point is, that while a boy learns he can be a husband, a father, and a doctor, lawyer, or the president of the United States, a girl learns she must be a wife and a mother first, and anything else only if she has the time or desperately needs the money. (You're allowed, of course, to get a job or think about a career, but nobody takes it as seriously as they do men's work, right? I mean, after all, you're just going to get married or at least have babies anyway, especially since everyone knows a woman isn't a real woman unless she has a man and children.) It's interesting, with the United States worrying about family values and how many children are in day care, that it does not seem often to be suggested that fathers stay home with their babies and give up what they have worked hard for.

Another point is, that while boys are brought up to please other people some of the time and please themselves some of the time (that's called setting up one's own standards, initiative, creativity, masculinity, aggressiveness), you are brought up to please other people — first your parents, then your teachers, then boys, then your husband, and then, so you don't get out of practice, your children. And you're supposed to please them all of the time. (That's called charm.) The reason for charm is so that when you find yourself (perhaps besides holding down a job) doing dishes, scrubbing floors, changing diapers, and all those other mindless, boring, repetitive tasks, you will always seem to be happy. A smiling, happy servant produces less guilt in everyone else than a cranky one. Then you will not just be a housewife, but a happy housewife, which pleases everyone enormously.

Do you finally understand what is being done to you just because you are a girl? A system that divides up what girls are allowed to do from what boys are allowed to do or makes rules for how girls have to behave and how boys have to behave is called a sex-role system. Or just sexism. The role you play in life, says a sexist society, is determined not by your own unique individuality, your own talents and ambitions, but by whether you happen to be a male or a female. A sexist society says a female is less intelligent, inferior, and has to learn to be passive, dependent, gentle, obedient, supportive, motherly; and a boy is more intelligent, superior, and has to learn to be active, independent, aggressive, brave, competitive, successful. A sexist society brings up its girls to have babies and do housework and take lower-paying jobs, work it calls less important, inferior to the work boys will do. A sexist society insists that the physical difference between being male and female (which makes an important difference only in making love and making babies) should also prevent half the human race from developing in areas that have nothing whatever to do with sex.

The Second Wave of the women's liberation movement that reached a peak between 1965 and 1975, feminism, an idea that has gone on for thousands of years, represents women's battle against sexism and all it stands for. We're in the Third Wave now in the nineties in the struggle against unequal pay, discrimination in educational and job opportunities, and the unfair legal restrictions on women's rights. The struggle is for day-care centers where children can be well taken care of while women work. The struggle is against sexist upbringing, which is as unfair to boys by forcing them to live up to ideals of masculinity, as it is to girls in forcing them to live up to ideals of femininity. But mostly, women's liberation is an ongoing battle against the enforced making of every woman primarily into a wife, a mother, a housekeeper, a second-class citizen. We have to ask, why didn't the women's liberation movement entirely work? With laws pretty much in place about sex discrimination and harassment and equal opportunity and pay both in schools and in the workplace, why has so much not changed for girls and women? Why do we continue in second place?

If self-reliance, and not self-pity, is the foundation of any revolution, any change, where is our self-reliance!

Tired of being inferior? Read on.

Section One

THE WAY IT IS

Growing Up A Girl

From the beginning it goes wrong. Even in the hospital nursery — which should be full of baby human beings, *all* of whom have the potential to grow into something special — they've already started handing the ribbons out. Pink for you, blue for the kid in the next crib.

If you are a boy, you're going to go out into the world and do something; you will learn independence, grow into maturity, and find your identity through your work.

If you are a girl, you won't actually *do* anything as seriously as a boy. You'll go on being a girl, and sooner or later, nature will take its course.

The sex roles have been handed out. A boy has to do and do and do to constantly prove his masculinity. And a girl isn't allowed to do anything too much or she will disprove her femininity. It isn't really fair to either sex. Although even if it's rougher on boys to begin with, it pays off later. Because at least boys can choose their destiny; the destiny of girls, whether they work or not, is always the same. Pick up a mop, have a baby, and join the parade.

Training begins early. It has to. Contrary to the fact that for thousands of years people have thought that girls were born intellectually inferior to boys, studies have shown that girls and boys are born intellectual equals. So, society, while it encourages a boy to grow, has to put a lot of pressure on a girl to keep her from growing. It isn't easy. Human beings, all human beings, have a need to grow that is just as basic to their nature as eating and sleeping. But there you are; you're a girl, and you have to be trimmed down to size.

In infancy and the early childhood years, psychologists have noted that boys are more physically active and aggressive than girls, while girls have greater verbal skills and a better understanding of their environment and relationship to the people around them. This means that boys act in ways society calls bad or more obnoxious than girls, and girls, because of their early understanding of what is expected of them, learn the pleasure of having other people's approval. One result of this is that by the time children are four or five, a boy has already learned to look to himself for approval, to develop a sense of himself in the outer, real world, to value himself in terms of his own achievement rather than through somebody else's approval. A girl is not forced into this position. All she has to do, which she can do very well because of her lesser aggression and her excellent analytical skills, is to conform to what is expected of her and go on being everybody's darling, lovable, pretty little lady. Progressively, she will move into her teens to value affiliation rather than achievement, popularity more than accomplishment, her attractiveness to others rather than to herself.

There is another important factor among these early parental attitudes toward young children. Although all infants and toddlers are dependent, boys are taught early not to cry, not to lean, to stand on their own two feet. Not girls, though. Our dependency is encouraged and rewarded. The lessons in sex roles are learned from the beginning. Boys are pressured to be active, to give up their childish ways, to earn their masculinity, to seek a sense of themselves in relation to the world. Girls are not pressured to prove anything. They are girls, and that is enough. Because of their ability to learn how to please and the rewards they get for pleasing others (with the media's junk values filling airways and cyberspace, 'pleasing' is based on being sexy [lookism] and on being helplessly skinny little girlish or helplessly plump little girlish as some blacks, Latinos, and Mediterranean cultures prefer [sexism]), they remain forever dependent on other people's values instead of forming their own. There's mommy's and daddy's good girl!

Okay. Now that you've been taught to lean on other people's approval instead of developing your own confidence and your own values, what else are you being taught and how?

One of the ways children are taught who they are and what they are supposed to do is through the kinds of activities they are given, or applauded for, or scolded for.

Boys are expected to run, jump, explore, climb, fight, get dirty, and take chances with their physical safety.

Ever heard fathers on the subject of their sons?

"Youngest kid on the block, and he can lick them all."

"Fell off his bike three times, but he never stopped trying. Didn't cry, either."

"Dirty? (Chuckle.) You never saw a kid so dirty. Took us a week to get him clean again."

Girls, on the other hand, are expected to be ladies. That includes sitting still as much as possible, being pretty, staying clean, and taking an interest in housekeeping, clothes, serving other people, clothes, babies, clean floors, baking cookies, clothes, clothes, and clothes.

Ever heard mothers on the subject of their daughters?

"I tell you, her brownies are better than mine. And good with the little ones?"

"Cute? There she was with her little dust rag, following me around the house."

"She was so proud of how pretty she looked in her new party dress, she didn't get a speck of dirt on it."

What all this accomplishes is twofold: it teaches a girl her place (behind a mop) and gives her an image (gorgeous). If this is kept up long enough, a girl will grow up to be that perfect specimen — a beautiful domestic servant. What else happens is that already her intellect is being damaged. The ability to cope and the capacity to think through problems are developed when children are allowed to solve things for themselves. Girls are so much more restricted (on the grounds that they are more fragile in a violent world, that they may be hurt, raped, generally spoiled for the marriage market) than boys, that they do not learn as early as boys, if ever, to cope with the world.

Children also learn about themselves through the toys they are given to play with. There he is with his football, his chemistry set, his building blocks, his trains, cars, and planes (he, after all, can choose single-mindedly to be a Michael Jordan, an Einstein, an architect, a test pilot); and there you are with your dolls, dishes, a miniature broom (not much choice of a future there). I don't say that little girls aren't given baseball gloves. But how many hours does daddy spend burning those fast balls into his little girl's glove compared to the hours he spends with her brother? And I don't say that now and then a little boy doesn't go to a tea party. But have you ever heard tell that his father bragged about it at the poker table?

No matter how you look at it, boys are trained early to develop healthy and adventurous spirits, while girls are trained to be dependent, and obedient, to curb their interests, and stay at home.

Interests. Now there's a good word. All children are born curious about everything. But that doesn't last very long. By the time girls are two or three, certainly no later than six or seven, they are generally told very specifically what they are and are not interested in. Boys are interested in how frogs jump, how engines run, how computers work, where the North Pole is or Mars. But girls are not supposed to be scientists, engineers, or space explorers, despite the fact that today many of them are. (You've even heard your mother take pride in explaining how unmechanical she is.) Girls are supposed to be far more interested in how to clean the house with the new vacuum cleaner (never mind how it works.)

The end of it all, of course, is that having been convinced that you have no interest in the real, outside world of doing and building and working, you are then told that, because you have no such interests, you are somehow inferior and not very bright. This doesn't matter, naturally, because you are pretty and will one day marry a bright, superior man. It's enough to make you scream, if you think about it long enough.

But we haven't finished with the arsenal yet. Other heavy guns are rolled out to keep you in your place. Think about the stories you were told when you were little. In most of them the boys were self-reliant achievers, with goals and a life of their own. Not the girls. The girls were childish, helpless little things whose only reward and safety lay in marriage.

Take Disney's *Snow White* as an example. (Mostly, you'll notice, we have European-American stories written mostly by men in school books, in movies, and on television, but there are Hispanic-American equivalents and African-American and Asian-American stories with girls just like *Snow White*.) Life with her stepmother was no bed of roses (even without today's crack, cockroaches, dysfunction, and divorce). But does she take off, as a boy would have done, to build herself a house somewhere and try her hand at farming or dragon-catching? Not Snow White. She hangs around complaining a lot and singing pop songs about a handsome prince until the huntsman explains he's been ordered to kill her and she better get out in a hurry. Now does she stomp over the nearest horizon to seek her fortune? Don't be silly. She races hysterically into the woods looking for a new domestic setup. She finds one all right. It's perfect for a feminine little girl. Not one, but seven men to wash, dust, and cook for. Does she ever say, "Wouldn't it be fun if I helped with the mining?" Never. But oh, those pies she bakes. And after all her troubles, what's her reward in the end? A career? An achievement? An interesting life? Of course not. A man with the biggest palace in the neighborhood, with enough housework to keep her busy the rest of her days. (Compare this to the fun Robin Hood had, or King of the Watusi, or Mowgli in the *Jungle Book*.)

And then there's television. Television tells you a lot about the roles of men and women. On television, it's mostly men who run around and do things. Women either wait for the men to come home, or if they're really clever, they help the men out a little. (If there is a female hero, she still worries about her femininity.) But it's the commercials that really get you. Boys are shown with laboratories, racing cars, or games that imitate the adult working world. Girls are shown with dolls that need a million dresses (to look gorgeous). Or with their hair being cream rinsed (to look gorgeous). (Do let me remind you that gorgeous is not an intelligent career no matter what anybody tells you.) Or else they are helping their mothers with the housework. (Let me also remind you that while housework has to be done, it is not stimulating, and it is definitely not enough to keep you going for a lifetime even if you do it for pay. Also, it can be done equally well by men.) Or else they are shown playing mother to baby dolls. (Babies are fun, they can only be birthed by women, they are stimulating, but when they grow up and go away, you still have half your life to live.)

You have not even entered first grade yet (no point in discussing day care, nursery school, and kindergarten where, as at home and in books and on television, there are boy things to do and girl things to do), and already you have begun to appreciate the fact that you are not being brought up, as a boy is, to be a wage earner and provider and a lot more. You are being brought up to be a wife and mother, and any more is just extra. You are not being brought up to be a complete human being who uses herself to the fullest of her capacities. You are brought up to serve and support other human beings and to deny a lot of your own potential.

So far, it's been psychological murder. But what till you get to school.

Girls In School

Everybody knows that the older girls get, the dumber they get. In grammar school, girls get much better grades than boys in all subjects, including arithmetic and science. In junior high school, girls do less well, especially in math and the sciences (boy stuff, right?). In high school, most girls' marks have dropped in most subjects (though the level is still higher than boy's marks, especially in all-girls' schools). And by the time girls get to college, many of them have practically given up trying.

Why?

Why does the girl child, who matures so quickly, who starts out so bright, suddenly stop growing mentally, and not only stop, but go backward? Why, oh why, when we were winning the race in the fifth grade, did so many of us suddenly slow down in the seventh, and then by the tenth grade decide to stop running altogether?

Does our intelligence fail? No.

Do we suddenly, in the bloom of our youth, get tired? Not likely.

Are they putting something in our food? Doubtful. (Although sometimes it does seem like a slow poison.)

What's being poisoned is not our minds or our bodies, but our will to succeed. Little by little, we are taught to be afraid of success. We are taught not to compete. We are taught not to be aggressive. The reason? If you are successful, competitive, and aggressive, you are told, boys won't like you.

(This is nonsense. Interesting boys like interesting girls.)

The real difficulty is that it is the need to succeed, not just at skills but at understanding this sometimes cruel and always complicated and demanding life, that sharpens and encourages intelligence. It is the need to make something out of your life that makes people work hard and well, and not just the outer life, but the inner life also. (You can be a great doctor or lawyer, and have a boring, narrow, prejudiced inner life.)

What happens to girls is that, after the early years of grammar school, society takes away the normal need to do the best you can, the normal assertiveness of every human being, the normal need to succeed, and replaces all of this by emphasizing that girls would be better off — more *feminine* — if they failed, or at least if they did a lot less well than boys. It's not only sad, it's a crime.

This devaluation of girls (they are called on much less in class, and when they vie for attention from the teacher or parents, they are called unladylike — you know, the boys-will-be-boys-stuff-but-a-girl-must-be-good-and-we-all-know-work-is-more-important-to-boys) tells girls that boys are just all-around more important to the world than girls are.

I once heard a ninth-grade girl say wistfully to a friend, "I used to want to be a biologist. I got pretty good marks in science, too. But then my other said boys don't like girls who are too brainy, so I don't study so much anymore, and my marks have dropped."

Her friend nodded in understanding. "My mother says men don't like it if you do anything too well. She says men like to win all the time, and if you want a husband, you have to learn how to lose. It isn't fair. I hate losing just as much as they do."

Some books separate out parents from society. But we are all society. And what society wants is for you to fit in, be like everybody else, not make waves or changes, be *like them*. Don't. It's a dead end. Which doesn't mean break laws or mess around. It means pay attention to the right things to do so you can have a meaningful life.

Many psychologists (mostly men), including Freud, have said that there is something missing in girls that boys have. They have said we lack the same intelligence, the same drive, the same capacities, and that these lacks are what make girls unable to work well, to compete well, to accomplish important things. It is these lacks that make us inferior to men, that make us second-class citizens.

The truth is, girls don't *lack* anything, not intelligence, not ability, not drive. We are simply told to forget about them. We are told to forget about them by the men who like to go on pretending they are superior and by the women who are brain-washed into helping the men pretend, or who just want to be taken care of and stand on a man's feet instead of standing on their own.

Remember, when you were in the first, second, third grades, even beyond, how it was all right to be smart? It was easy then. Nobody bothered you then about competing with boys. (At home, of course, you were already role-playing; you helped with the dishes while your brother learned to farm, work on the car, survive the streets, or recite the names of football heroes.) But at school, even though you sewed while he took shop, and you didn't always play the same games in gym, at least nobody bothered your head. Both sexes were rewarded for academic achievement. (Although a lot of schoolbooks still tend to have sexist pictures and texts with girls in kitchens and boys swinging bats, with history stories featuring heroic, mostly white males and passive females or no females at all.)

Yet girls are set up to do very well in school. At home, they've already learned to depend on other people's approval rather than personal confidence (now they get teacher's approval for sitting still as well as mommy's). They've learned to conform (sit still if everybody else is sitting still); obey (enjoy getting pats on the head for sitting still); and be passive (sit still so they won't get dirty, won't be noisy, won't be unfeminine, etc.). As it happens, this works out very well. You have to be able to sit still if somebody is going to teach you anything at all.

It also happens that with the extra maturity girls have, the better verbal skills and perceptual skills, they learn admirably well what they are expected to learn. And grammar schools are still very feminine institutions where the teachers, most of whom are women, value exactly what little girls are all about.

Your brothers, at this point, were too twitchy (they ran around too much), too aggressive (they talked back), and too independent (they cared more about objective achievements like winning a race than the approval of grownups and good marks).

So you did well in grammar school. In the area of academic achievement, you were not only allowed to be competitive, aggressive, and successful, you were rewarded for it. Even in athletics at this point in your life, nobody bothered you if you ran faster, climbed higher, or threw a better baseball. By the time you were in the sixth grade, you were probably feeling pretty cocky. You could try hard and be rewarded by success, not just praise. You felt you could cope with the world and enjoy it, as a person and a girl.

Then all of a sudden something changed. You started growing breasts, rounding at the hips, looking like a woman instead of a little girl. And with that, everybody's mind about you and how you were supposed to behave changed, too.

Suddenly, you were no longer a regular person doing her best. You were a female, and you weren't supposed to do too well anymore.

Sexism, role playing according to which sex you are, had begun to interfere with your natural abilities, your natural competitiveness, your natural pleasure in success.

Now that you've grown you're interested in boys (and even if you're not yet, or you're a lesbian and never will be interested, everybody tells you you should be), what advice are you are given? Is it:

"Boys are marvelous creatures, someday you may even want to marry one of them, but in the meantime remember you are a human being first and human beings need to grow and be as fully developed as their abilities will allow them?"

Never!

The advice you are given, if not openly, by general social pressure, is, "Slow down, cookie. Boys don't want any competition from you. All you have to be from here on in is sexy enough to catch one of them. Never mind the books now, the good marks, the basketball practice. Concentrate on makeup, short skirts, a thin body, the right skin tone, and man-catching facial expressions." In other words, get out of the way and let the real people run the world.

Now you'd think any self-respecting girl would blink a couple of times in surprise, give a couple of hoots of laughter, and go on with whatever she was doing. (Switch it around and imagine telling a thirteen- or fourteen-year-old boy to give up his computer or his basketball hoop in order to concentrate on his looks so he could catch a wife.) But girls don't laugh away the advice and pressures to go on with whatever they are doing. They listen and obey.

The reason they listen is because they have not been given enough self-respect, because they have had all that early training in dependency on other people's approval. They start out by being trained to need mommy's approval; after that, they achieve well in grade school because of the rewards for this 'good' behavior that comes from others (rather than for achievement's own sake). Now society (society is everybody — parents, teachers, friends, peers, your gang, the other gangs—you yourself, if you're not careful), society says, "Stop competing with the boys. Compete for the boys, if you want approval." So, in order to be approved of, girls stop competing. Really cool girls let their grades drop, drop out altogether, and stop doing anything at all.

The result is that while boys grow more and more afraid of failing (boys have other problems, but this book is about girls), girls grow more and more afraid of succeeding. And unless you live your life on your own feet, you have no confidence in yourself. Therefore, girls go on depending on others rather than themselves for a sense of worth.

Not only at home and in society does this happen. It even happens in school, which is the one place all people should be given the chance to develop their capacities, their interests, their purposes in the world.

But both in courses and in counseling, girls get the short end of the stick.

By junior high and high school (this coincides with the time you begin to be whistled at and grabbed at and otherwise degraded as body parts instead of a whole human being), you can forget about equality in sports. Even if you haven't been separated from boys before, you're separated from them now.

The excuse is that boys are faster, stronger, and that girls aren't good enough to be on the same playing field with them. Even if we accept that (although in any class, *some* girls are better athletes than *some* boys), how come girls aren't equally encouraged to develop their bodies? Most of the time it's the boys' teams and the boys' sports that get funded and clapped for, not the girls'. (In this area, as in the workplace, the laws for equality may be in place — but you can't legislate attitudes, and it's attitude we suffer from.)

Courses, naturally, are even worse than sports. Why are the boys encouraged to go into technical training, printing, carpentry, computer programming (this is changing, so that girls can make better secretaries), machine shop (lots of women work in factories, go into the publishing business, build furniture, excel at computer technology), while the girls end up with cooking, home-making, and child-care classes? The schools just seem to assume that all boys have more talent for chemistry labs, electronics, mechanical drawing, machine parts (not true; girls' aptitudes have been tested and are just as good as boys'); and that all girls are just fascinated with chocolate pudding, laundry detergents, and diapering bottoms (ridiculous!). It's all part of the plot to keep you in your place or at least teach you where your place is.

Math, the sciences, government, economics, engineering are supposed to be boy stuff. (If you are interested in these things, better not make a point of it, and if you know the answer in class, have the grace to be meek about it front of the boys. Not that you'll get called on as often as the boys anyway — studies show that teachers call on boys far more often than girls. It's all right, however, to be interested in literature and the arts, home economics, secretarial studies. This is feminine stuff (and heaven help the boy who happens to be talented in oil painting, ballet dancing, or writing poetry).

Heaven also help the African-American girl, the Asian-American girl, the Native-American girl interested in something besides male European-American culture — she will be left with very little in school.

Obviously, this is all ridiculous. Talents and abilities have nothing to do with sex; people of either sex can be capable in any area of work and study. But anyone's ability can be murdered by neglect or downright disapproval.

With the courses you take comes the counseling. The major attitude seems to be, not that you are a human being with a definite talent or interest (you may have been brainwashed out of this by now anyway) but that you are a female, and females are supposed to do female-like work (until you get married when you will be sent to the kitchen where all females belong). What you will find out is that female work, the nursing and teaching professions, secretarial and kitchen work, all the nurturing work of humanity, is the lowest-paid and most undervalued work of all.

Not that there is anything wrong with these professions. Being a teacher is probably the most honorable, gratifying, and most necessary profession of all. Even men understand the rewards in the nursing profession now. The thing is, though, you aren't given much choice. Everybody encourages girls to go into the "mothering" professions (same old role), and there is still less encouragement for the girl who wants to be a surgeon, a judge, a scientist, than for a boy.

And if you like working with your hands or fixing things, nobody says to you, "be a carpenter, or open your own garage." They tell you to be a dress designer or teach arts and crafts. A scant 16 percent of currently employed scientists are female; the numbers of women pursuing degrees in science and engineering are dropping, especially in advanced physics and math. Part of the problem, of course, is that boys, who have not been taught that girls' brains are as good as their own, do not work well with girls in science lab groups either in school or later on in the workplace. Except in all-girls' schools, confidence drops, and with confidence, achievement. Girls just give up trying. Even gifted girls, to win the approval of teachers and boys, begin to act stupid, helpless, and silly.

A nd of course these days you are dealing with more than school in school. You're dealing earlier than ever, as early as eight, nine, ten years old, with violence and terror: The terror of guns and gangs, drugs and alcohol, unwanted sex, never mind unwanted pregnancy, STD's,

AIDS, is no longer confined to inner city schools. Violence, addiction, racism, and just the trauma of being a teenager are attacking you as well as sexism. And it's everywhere.

So when you hear that you are dumber than a boy, less ambitious than a boy, inferior in sports or in class, you can just tell them that if they hadn't hung all that femininity around your neck, all that insecurity and lack of confidence, the general terror of just having to face being a teenage girl, you might have outraced any boy on your block.

Girls And Boys

In spite of the problems (and believe it, both sexes have problems), it's nice to be a girl. And one of the nicest feelings, if you are a girl, is to be with a boy you like and who likes you.

But don't you sometimes wish the relationship between you and boys could be a little more natural, a little less fixed in its rules about who has to do and say what, a little more *human*?

Take a quick look at the dating process. What happens?

Weeks before you even get to the point of an actual date, you have spent a lot of time trying to look adorable. (He has been trying to impress you by making the football team, getting the lead in the school play, or being elected president of his class — which means that even if he doesn't get you, he will have achieved something anyway.) If you don't get him, all you'll be left with is a new eyebrow piercing, an extra sweater, and a crushed ego. But since you're not supposed to compete and achieve anything or you'll scare him off, you're left with looking adorable. Looking adorable and hanging around, that is.

Because heaven forbid you should make the first move. You like him, you make a pretty shrewd guess he likes you, but there is absolutely nothing you can do about it. Girls are freer since the women's movement of the late sixties and early seventies and the two-career lives of eighties' and nineties' marriages and the greater number of single-parent (mostly mothers) families — but still! Believe it or not, people still think if *you* ask *him*, you're chasing him, setting a trap for him. Why? All you want to do is maybe take a walk or go to a movie, not cook him for dinner.

All right. You have followed rules one and two — looking cool and waiting around — and you have finally batted your new eyelashes enough to attract his attention, and he asks you to that movie. The next rule is that he has to pick you up at your house. Even if the movie is nearer his house. Even if you have a car, and he doesn't. Even if he doesn't have much money, and the extra carfare hurts. (The boy-picks-up-the-girl rule is less rigid than it used to be in many communities, but a lot of people still consider it uncouth for a girl to pick up a boy, or for a girl to pay taxi or bus fare.)

Which brings us to the subject of who pays: for the carfare, for the movie, for the food. You may have more money that week or in general or at least enough money to split expenses. No matter. He's the boy, and usually he pays. There are several psychologically damaging things about this rule besides the fact that it isn't fair for the boys to have to spend their money all the time. The boys, who pay, get to feeling an edge of superiority — people who control the money arrangements always do — and girls end up with the feeling they've been bought and paid for and they'd better be nice, a distinctly inferior and childlike position to be stuck in. Also, because he's paying, you have to go along with what he wants to do, generally, not what you might like to do. (Just out of curiosity, how many times have you let a boy kiss and touch you because he spent so much money on you that evening? Would you have allowed him what he wanted if you had paid for the evening?)

So far, you've obeyed all the rules of femininity, and he's obeyed all the rules of masculinity (no matter what your true needs as human beings). Now how does the evening go?

He, being the masculine one, leads the way. He may do all the talking, or he may expect you to entertain him. The choice is not usually yours, it's his. If he has opinions on any subject, he will expect you to accept most of them (he's smarter, and anyway you're not supposed to compete with him). You're also supposed to flatter him (your mother told you to build up a man's ego) in as many ways as possible.

Remember, he lives in a world that has told him boys are more valued than girls, where in India, Africa, China, in the Middle East, only boys are prized and girls are even sometimes killed or left under a rock. Until the world changes its attitudes and gender is a matter of indifference, boys will be bullies because we have told them they are the preferred sex. If you are at the top of the social heap as boys are, you always feel you have a right to have your own way and the inferiors (you) should be honored to be in your presence. You job, of course, to help remind him of this if he forgets it, or his superiority needs shoring up like all castles built on shaky ground. This is called being feminine. Other ways to be feminine are to giggle at his jokes, to behave as if you couldn't cross a street by yourself, and to be built like a California beach bunny or an African goddess. (He, if he is properly masculine, will have the grace to be at least six feet tall, be able to lift twice his own weight, and will be planning to be as rich as you are beautiful.)

If you're going to a party (to the beach, a club, a rave, to drive to park somewhere, even just down Main Street), what do you want to bet the girls will get to cope with the food (you're good at details like that), and the boys will sit around talking to each other the way they almost never talk to you (real conversation can only be carried on among men).

If you've got a long-term relationship going, how much time do you spend following him and his friends around compared to the time he spends following you and your friends around? And how much time do you spend clapping for him compared to the clapping he does for you? Of course, he thinks you're pretty. But what else? While you tell him he's a marvelous basketball player (mechanic, guitarist, all-around-hero) what does he tell you? That you write brilliant compositions, quadratic equations, lab reports? Or are you the one who cooks good, looks good, and will someday be a terrific mother.

And speaking of your futures, how do you speak of your futures? He's going to be what — an electrician, a lawyer, a businessman, a politician? You take it seriously and encourage him. But you tell him you're going to have a career, and unless it's nursing, teaching, or maybe fashion-designing, you'll see on his face anything from mild shock to hilarity. Jobs are okay, to help out or fill time or share bills even after you're married, but a serious commitment to a serious lifetime work? That makes him nervous. Marriage and maternity and wearing pretty clothes should be enough fulfillment for you. (Ask him sometimes if being a husband and a father and a new pair of jeans would be enough for him.)

The funny thing is that there are boys who really do like cooking and taking care of the children, who might well make excellent housekeepers. But they are too hung up on their masculinity to admit it. You may swing a microscope better, and he may sing a better lullaby, but unfortunately each of you is stuck in the machinery of sexism. It just isn't human, any of it.

The two saddest results of the double-sex standard are that: one, girls are too often kept from useful work and from being people as well as wives and mothers; and, two, the relationship between boys and girls becomes very difficult, especially for girls. Because a boy is taught that he is strong, and the leader, and a girl is weaker, and the follower; because they both learn that his work is more important than her work, that he controls the money while she waits for handouts or lower pay; because of all this, they end by agreeing that a girl is not as good as a boy.

What this leads to, of course, is that since you aren't his equal, the two of you can't really be friends. Therefore, sex usually forms the only basis of the relationship between you. This gives a lot of girls the sneaking feeling they're being used instead of enjoyed as people. It also means that if you aren't in love with a boy, or he isn't mad about you, it's very hard just to be friends. And when boys get to the point where girls only mean sex, you can hardly walk down the street or through the school halls without whistles, remarks, or worse. Being attractive is lovely. Being pestered to death, grabbed at, called slut if you do and lesbian if you don't put out, makes girls and women feel violated, depressed, and scared. In a 1992 survey of girls in grades 2-12, 89% of the respondents said they had been targets of unwanted sexual gestures, looks, or comments, or had their bodies grabbed or their pants pulled down, sometimes "just for fun."

Even more than the hidden school curriculum (the open curriculum is reading, writing, arithmetic) that restricts and diminishes and sometimes denies girls' study and work experience, there is the problem of twisting girls' natural sexual desire into something ugly and making her conscious of sexual exploitation and abuse. It is in adolescence that girls learn their bodies are not their own to enjoy. Gang initiation is an extreme example, when girls go through "training," hazing. Boys are "jumped in" — either beat up or asked to commit a crime. Girls, though they may be jumped in the same way, are often also asked to prove their loyalty by having sex with the males in the gang. In a notable 1993 case, a number of girls came to a Planned Parenthood office in Texas asking for HIV tests — they had been forced to have unprotected sex to jump in a gang. The girls learned sexual victimization the hard way. But even without such hard lessons, even among the girls just trying to get through school and learn, the sex pressure is on. Throughout the generations, one thing has never changed: if you sleep with boys, you're a slut; if you don't, you may never be asked out again. And throughout the generations, it has often slipped adult minds to inform girls their sexual desire can be as strong as a boy's — and sometimes we get pregnant because we don't want to stop to remember about safe sex either.

Aside from such big problems caused by having to be feminine, how about the small ones? What is all that business about girls being more girlish if they sit a certain way, drink a glass of water a certain way, run a certain way, wear miserably uncomfortable high heels and tight skirts? Why should it all matter so much? A more important question is, why do girls put up with it all?

The answer is that a part of you enjoys it. (People never do anything for very long unless it satisfies *something* inside them.) Part of you enjoys being small and weak while he is big and strong. Part of you enjoys being the follower behind his leadership. Part of you enjoys the fact that he is supposed to know much more about the world than you do. Part of you even enjoys being put in your place, being inferior. (Think about this; sadly, it's true.)

There are reasons why part of you enjoys it. Sometime around the beginning of adolescence you were told that the only true reward in life for a woman was catching and marrying a man, and that being feminine, submissive and weak, not strong and accomplished, was the only way to get one. So by behaving in this feminine way, you get two gold stars: you get the man, and you get everybody's approval for having gotten him. When you know you're behaving in a way that everybody is going to applaud, your need for approval (because you're conditioned to be a girl) is going to make you enjoy behaving in such a way.

What nobody ever tells you is that grownups get married because it's a nice way to live for both men and women, that it happens naturally, that you don't have to work so hard to make sure it happens.

Another reason girls accept an inferior position to boys is that they need boys so badly. Girls, as we have seen, learn to value themselves only if other people love and value them. In the beginning a little girl looks to her parents for approval and love, then she looks to her teachers. Eventually, as she grows up, she transfers her need for approval to boys. Most girls never learn to look to themselves, to rely on their own achievements to make them feel important. So girls go on needing boys because they can't afford to lose what they think of as their only source of love — that is, masculine approval.

Feeling inferior to boys is another reason girls put up with being treated as inferiors. If you're not encouraged to learn, after a while you're going to stop bothering. And if you stop bothering, you end up nowhere, being treated as if you were nobody. This is the result of what Mary Pipher calls our hyper-sexualized, media-saturated, girl-poisoning culture in her book *Reviving Ophelia*. You just can't feel like too much if you are prey to eating disorders, depression, addictions, self-mutilations, and a slight yearning to be dead half the time.

Being nobody is a terrible problem. But if your whole life is spent playing the role of "girl" how are you going to find out what you really are as a person, what you like, and what you don't like, what you're good at and what you're not, what you think and what you don't think? How often have you heard that a man is a girl's destiny, that you're supposed to wait until he hands you your future? He'll be somebody, and you'll end up as Mrs. Carpenter, or Mrs. Astronaut, or Mrs. Storeowner.

And believe it, being Mrs. Somebody is not the same as being somebody yourself. There's not much sense of personal identity in it and not much pride.

I'm not saying it isn't wonderful to be attractive and loved. I'm not even saying that every girl should go out and save the world.

What I am saying is that being attractive and loved isn't enough to make anybody happy forever, boy or girl, and that everybody, girls included, should be allowed the independence and sense of usefulness that comes with knowing how to earn a living at work one chooses to do, at being treated as an adult human being.

The thing is, if girls stopped playing dumb, there wouldn't be anybody left to make the boys feel smarter!

Women In College

Y ou will notice from the chapter title that the word "women" is used, not "girls." If you are old enough to get a job without parent-signed working papers, old enough to get married without parental permission, able enough to be responsible for yourself, you are entitled to be called a woman, not a girl. If you hear your mother and her friends, or the women of community organizations or at work, still referring to themselves as "girls," it is because they have gotten so little satisfaction or reward from maturity. They continue to strain backward toward the only triumphant time of their lives, those girlish years when they dated, caught, and married a man. Their image of themselves is still dependent and childlike; they still feed on their husbands (or wish they did) instead of on their own.

One of the most important moments in your life comes when you graduate from high school. Will you simply latch onto the nearest male as soon as possible and depend on him to provide you with your future? (Not entirely fair to a man, since it leaves him totally responsible for two and then more lives. And quite possibly dangerous for you, since a man can get sick, or die, want a divorce, or just leave. Or even if none of these things happen, you simply can't expect another human being to fill fifty or sixty years of your life with joy. You're going to have to manage to find some satisfaction on your own.

Nobody says it's easy. If, as a girl, you've had it rough in high school with unfair-to-girls courses or classroom treatment, bad counseling, and playing second fiddle to the boys, as a woman looking for equal work, equal pay, or higher education and better position, you're going to find it even rougher.

We haven't discussed the special problems of being African American, Latino, Asian American, or American Indian, because up until now the problems have been much the same for all girls, black, brown, yellow, white. From here on in, if you happen to be other than Caucasian as well as a woman, you can just about double the difficulties. You have to work against two handicaps: racism and sexism. You have two battles to fight: the first is alongside the black or brown man for racial equality; and the second battle, to be fought alongside sisters of all colors, is against five or ten thousand years of political and psychic oppression of women. (Anthropological studies note that there have been a number of primitive societies where inheritance is matrilineal and where women have had status. Among the American Hopi Indians of the Arizona desert, women are almost dominant. In some Australian aboriginal tribes, women are still dominant. Alas, this has never happened in a major civilization, however, so while it proves that the ability to rule is not an inherent characteristic of the male, we still haven't had a real chance at it.)

If you've managed to survive high school without trading in your pink ribbon for a vacuum cleaner (or even if you've got the vacuum cleaner and you're still bent on a larger life), you're going to have to work even harder to survive college with your head in one piece. There are few all-female higher sanctuaries left (the price of getting into the good-old-boys' clubs was letting the boys into the good-old-girls' clubs), so you're going to have to work hard to get into college.

Getting into college is still harder for women than for men. Women need higher grades for admission to many colleges and universities, especially if you want traditional male fields of study: veterinary medicine; engineering; advanced physics; that sort of thing. Official and unofficial quota systems for women are widespread. There are still universities known to state that admission of women on the freshman level will be restricted to those who are especially well qualified, and other universities with systems to make sure girls are never in the majority, in spite of the fact that in terms of grades and tests scores there are often more qualified females than males. Whatever women must do they must do twice as well as men to be thought half as good. ("Luckily, this is not difficult," is my favorite return, courtesy of a Canadian mayor named Charlotte Whitton.)

And the higher up you go on the educational ladder, the worse it gets.

Women have trouble being admitted to some graduate and professional training programs because of the ridiculous reasoning that "if a woman is not married, she will get married; if she is married, she will have children; if she has children, she cannot possibly be dedicated to a serious profession; if she has older children, she is too old to begin training." Men are not punished for getting married. Men are not punished because they become parents. Men are not told that having families means they aren't serious about their professions. Society doesn't limit men, but it punishes women simply for being women.

There are very few colleges and universities that make it easy for a woman who has children to study. There are not enough good day-care centers. There are not enough institutions with good advisory and support systems for women who must devote part of their time to domestic responsibilities.

Even worse, however, is what can happen to you at college or university once you are there. It can be intense psychological warfare.

I have heard hard-working young friends of mine repeat awful things their professors have said to them.

"What's a cute girl like you worrying her head over political science for?" (I can't figure out the logic of that one. Did he mean that if you're cute you are stupid, or if you're cute you *should* be stupid? Or did he mean that if you're cute, you're supposed to be living with some man and stop thinking altogether? Or did he mean only ugly people are interested in government and politics? At any rate, you can see the brilliance of his remark.)

"I know you do excellent work. I know your grades are high. But are you really serious about what you are doing?" (What kind of question is that? Why does anybody work hard unless they're serious about what they're doing?)

"You're only going to get married, what do you want with a Master's?" (Never occurred to him that she could get married and be a cosmologist, or be a cosmologist and a real person without getting married at all.)

"The mind of a woman is inferior to the mind of a man because women are too emotional to think clearly." (No comment on that one except to suggest that he's got the mind of a caveman, and you might answer with "ugh," if you ever hear the remark yourself.)

Aside from the put-downs about the quality of a woman's mind and the seriousness of her purposes, there are other even more difficult problems.

One truly great difficulty is the quality of women's education. In many universities, women are shunted off into the usual "feminine" courses such as English literature, the arts, education and child care, nursing, library training. (I'll repeat, that while these are most honorable professions, women should have as full a spectrum of choices as men.)

In *Shortchanging Girls, Shortchanging America*, a study done in the early 1990's by the American Association of University Women, the attention of the country was focused on the fact that twenty years after the passage of Title IX (the federal law banning sex discrimination in school programs), it was discovered that girls still receive an unequal education in our nation's schools.

Gender bias, feminization lowers the IQ points. Journalists like Peggy Orenstein (who wrote a book called *SchoolGirls* in 1994), the feminist writer Carolyn Heilbrun (who wrote, among other books, *Reinventing Womanhood* in 1979), point out over and over again that while girls start out equally smart and talented, there are almost no female role models. History is pretty much about men. While 90% of psychology students are female, the accepted theorists are mostly male. We read William Shakespeare because they never taught his sister Dramatic Arts. There has always been so much gender bias, girls have been pretty much feminized out of the independent nature it requires to fully participate in the life of the world. Women now earn a majority (54%) of U.S. college degrees. And they've integrated many graduate and professional programs that were long the domain of men. About 40% of all medical and law graduates now are female, up from fewer than one-tenth in 1970. Nearly 3 out of 4 married mothers were in the labor force by 1996, compared with half in 1970. BUT women still do two thirds of the housework and child care, and they still only earn 71% of men's earnings. *Why do we put up with this?*

In many colleges and universities, the training still isn't really practical. As you sit in the general courses your advisor has suggested that cover every imaginable liberal arts subject, it dawns on you slowly that you aren't being trained for anything. There are many educators who believe that a general liberal arts background is an excellent mind opener for everyone, men as well as women. The difference is that when men take liberal arts courses, they are told they will eventually concentrate in one field, perhaps take a higher degree in their specialization, become heads of university departments or university presses. But if a woman asks questions about her unspecialized courses, her future in the job market, she may get the answer I once got.

"Job market? We're not preparing you here for the job market. We're preparing you to be the kind of well-educated person who will make the sort of mother all children should have and the sort of wife who is most helpful to her husband."

(They were right about one thing. I had to take a secretarial course when I got out of college to get a job at all. As for being a wife and mother, I learned how to do that on my own. It would have been much more helpful if I had been trained to *do* something while I was in college and also to have been offered special courses in the special problems women face. Too much to ask in four years of college? I don't think so.)

Today, many once-liberal-arts-only colleges are offering practical courses like computer technology, partly because businesses demand it. Minority women particularly tend to take more career-track programs.

But still, too often in so many colleges and universities, women are given a sterile education that prepares them to do absolutely nothing satisfying in the real world. Forty percent of those with an aptitude for engineering, for instance, are women, but nothing like 40% of engineers are women. And too often women are counseled to enter fields that society considers feminine. The trouble with that is not that the work is not interesting or valuable, but that it is low in both status and pay.

Sex discrimination can take even more active forms than just discouragement. In Hillary Carlip's book *Girl Power*, a 1995 study and collection of writings of the abuse and shame and fury, joys and triumphs of girls 12-20, in which it becomes evident that young women are no longer willing to suffer passively and endure silently, she describes the Riot Grrrls, a network of angry revolutionaries who write and mail each other "zines," and hold workshops to go into their issues of fat, oppression, rape, racism, and sexuality.

Among the girls' discoveries is that one out of three women will be raped in her lifetime and four out of five rape victims know their attackers. But date rape, whether at high school levels or on university campuses or on military training bases is only one form of abuse. There is sometimes just punishment simply for being female. (There was a case of broken pelvises due to forced marches among female rookies at one military academy.) Everywhere there is discrimination against lesbians. And there is a lack of accommodation for women with disabilities that amounts to discrimination.

If part of the difficulty in getting the education you want and need is sex discrimination, the other part is what we have been discussing in the past few chapters — the bringing up of girls either to feel inferior or to act as if they were inferior in order to do the one thing that is expected of them: get married.

Many studies have shown that college women are *afraid* of success, afraid that if they do too well they will not be considered feminine and men won't like them. Many do get good grades, but they do not always take their commitment to their work seriously. They have to spend too much time when they are with men playing dumb, giving up their own identities to play the traditional sex role. So they end up by being the doctor's wife instead of the doctor *and* a wife.

Even those women whose parents have encouraged them to do well in school, to enter college to learn more, to develop themselves as human beings, often discover that what those same parents really had in mind was that college was a great place to find a husband. (Is this why 4 out of every 10 American women are pregnant by age 20, the highest ratio of any industrialized country — so that girls can prove to everyone they're real women?)

It's a sad moment for a woman who has worked hard to get into college, who has been rewarded for her academic achievement, when she trades in her mind, the possibility of an interesting career (or at least the ability to be financially independent), and her growth into a mature adult to restrict herself to being merely a wife, even a working wife, if that work does not satisfy her. If she gives up all she has achieved, she may end up being a girl forever, and never a woman.

P.S. Sorry for pounding the same dismal drum over and over — being a woman is a miraculous and beautiful incarnation on this earth. But the miracle and beauty often remain internal. The external conditions remain unusually difficult, sometimes servile, and often dangerous.

Women At Work

It's a man's world out there.

Don't let anybody kid you that secretly women have power over men (they don't), that women really hold the purse strings of the nation (they don't), that women are happier serving and helping men (they aren't).

These are just some of the fairy tales everybody uses to keep women content with second place. There is an old saying that behind every successful man, there is a woman. Sure there is — about five steps behind, like a foot-bound Chinese wife.

Suppose now you've got your high school or college diploma. You've traded in your blue jeans for a pair of decent slacks or a power suit. You've understood that:

1) all people, male and female, married or not married, who want self-respect, self-reliance, and maturity instead of a childish dependency on others must develop their own skills, whatever they are, and use them

2) three out of four women, married and mothers, are in the labor force, and more managers are women: 43% in 1995, up from 19% in 1970 (decades of fighting for equal opportunity are beginning to show, even though more women than men are likely to be poor due to 29% lower pay, to high birth rates, to being left worse off than men after divorce or widowhood)

3) work and marriage go very nicely together (that old nonsense about the family unity and strength being threatened if a woman works is just that — nonsense!)

4) nine out of ten women work at some point during their lives

5) even if women stay home to have babies, the average woman sends her last child off to school by the time she is thirty-five or forty, which still leaves about forty more years of her life to fill

Furthermore, you've understood that useful, valued work is necessary to everyone's mental health, that your brain is just as good as a man's brain, that your ability to do a job is the same as a man's.

You've understood all of this. You're ready to face the working world and look for a job. Let's see what you're going to find.

Well, actually, what you're going to find is a mess.

You're going to find a lot of the same stupid business you've been hit over the head with all your life. Just as in the sandbox the boys got to do the trucking, and the digging, and the building while you got to bring the juice and cookies on your tea set; just as in high school and college, while the boys talked about things going on in the world, you got trapped into conversations about the boys; in a business office, you'll find things haven't really progressed too far. Like all the people you've ever known — parents, teachers, friends, boyfriends, busdrivers, policemen — your employers will see you as a sex object, a baby maker, a wife-mother, even if you're not. They will see you as a helper, rather than a doer. They will see you as all the things they wish you were, even if you are not: passive, weak, too emotional, unable to cope with important jobs, obedient, and definitely inferior to men. And because employers see you this way, they will give you the least desirable, lowest-paying jobs, with the least possibility for advancement. (We can beat the situation, though. Women all over the world are not only legislating equality, but changing attitudes to go with it.)

It's still pretty rough, however.

For one thing, the world has the peculiar idea that it doesn't have to pay women as much money as men for doing the same job. On the average, as of 1995, women earn seventy-one cents for every dollar that men earn, says the Population Reference Bureau. This is compared to fifty-nine cents on general average in 1975. So decades of fighting for equal opportunity are beginning to pay off. But there is still pay inequality, for every kind of work from secretary to scientist. This continues to be true despite the aspirations of the Baby Boomers, the 1980's Yuppies, the Generation Xers. Annual average earnings (Bureau of the Census) by educational level, sex, race, Hispanic origin among men and women ages 18 and over in 1994:

	TOTAL	No HS Grad	HS Grad	Bachelor Degree	Advance Degree
Male	$32,000	$16,000	$25,000	$46,000	$67,000
Female	18,000	9,000	15,000	26,000	40,000
White	26,000	14,000	21,000	38,000	56,000
Black	19,000	13,000	16,000	31,000	48,000
Hispanic	18,000	14,000	17,000	29,000	52,000

There is an Equal Pay Act. It was passed in 1963. And it was supposed to make it illegal to discriminate against women. In some cases, companies were forced to see that certain women got equal pay, even retroactively. But there are two main problems with the Equal Pay Act. The government doesn't have enough staff to look into every situation. And the Equal Pay Act does not cover women in professional, executive, or administrative jobs.

Besides the unequal pay, women also suffer from being put into less-skilled jobs, where the pay is low and there isn't much hope of advancement either.

Ask any woman lawyer how much harder it is for her to earn a partnership than a male lawyer. Ask any woman in banking, in computer technology, any woman veterinarian, surgeon, architect, factory or office manager, pilot or politician, and she will tell you she not only has to be twice as good as a man, but also she will often earn half as much.

We could go on with these numbers, but they would only prove the same obvious point. The job scene for women, and to a strangely high degree in the United States, is unhealthy, unequal, and unfair.

Women work for the same reasons men do — for money, for the satisfaction of doing a good job, to give purpose, meaning, direction to their lives. Women therefore ought to have the same opportunities.

There are two main reasons women are not given the same chance as men. Men are prejudiced against women. And women are prejudiced against themselves. As children, they were all taught to think of females as less valuable than males.

In a New York school, a poll was taken. The question was, "Would you vote for a woman to be president of the United

States?" It wasn't too surprising that most of the boys flatly answered, "no." What was surprising was that many of the girls answered the same way. Their answers included statements such as, "politics are for men," and "men have better minds for that sort of thing," and "men are stronger, so they should be the leaders."

While it is perfectly true that men think badly of most women's mental abilities, it is also true that women have a bad image of themselves. In many offices, if there is an opening for promotion, it will more likely be given to a man, "because a man needs the money more." (Why? With the rising divorce rates, more women are heads of households than ever before.) Or, "because one of these days she'll get married, have babies, and quit." (Who says so? As we mentioned, 3 out of 4 married moms were in the labor force in 1996.) But the more important point here is that not only do men treat us this way, but also that we accept it. We have been trained for so many years to take second place, that often we don't even fight back.

Too many women are successful in too many fields for men to be able to say any longer that women don't have the brains to do a job well. Opportunities may be difficult to come by, but there are famous women who are in politics, who are on the New York Stock Exchange, who run advertising agencies, who are leading physicists, anthropologists, corporation directors, senators, writers, retailers, publishers, sales managers, doctors, and lawyers. What men have taken to saying now is, "maybe she has the brains, but she isn't emotionally stable enough," or "women are difficult to deal with," or "any woman who's *that* successful has to be a little nutty, (or too aggressive, or less than a woman, and so forth)."

It isn't easy working in what is so far still a man's world. You'll either get the worst jobs, or if you get a good one, you'll have to fight twice as hard as a man to keep it. If you are a black woman or belong to any ethnic minority, you can double the difficulty. (Many minority women workers are in service work, and earning at or below poverty level incomes.)

You'll be watched more closely, and you'll get a lot more criticism. Men bond and band together; women have not yet really learned to form networks to support one another. Too many successful women become honorary males instead of reaching out to help other women. While there are some organizations for business and professional women like AWED for women entrepreneurs, too few women in corporations find and help one another.

You'll be left out of important business meetings and barred from business clubs and then criticized for not knowing what's going on.

You'll be insulted and belittled if you don't act "feminine" and then either sexually harassed or held back from promotion or both if you do act "feminine."

If you have children, people will worry that you're going to quit your job or have child care problems. If you don't have children, they'll call you unnatural.

Because many women still say they are working "only until I get married," "just to help out for a while," "just to put my husband through school," women's image in the working world remains tarnished. The fact is that statistics show that women hold their jobs longer than men do, now. (So don't let some male boss tell you women's job-turnover rate is higher — it isn't.) Also, women take off less time for illness than men, including time taken off to have babies.

Another criticism leveled at women is their lack of assertiveness in the workplace. Here, white middle-class women who are floundering in contradictory messages of assertiveness and compliance, of achievement and containment, could learn much from their black sisters. Writer Toni Morrison, Nobel Prize winner, has said, in Claudia Tate's interview with her in *Black Women Writers At Work*, "Aggression is not as new to black women as it is to white women. Black women seem able to combine the nest and the adventure. They don't see conflicts in certain areas as do white women. They are both harbor and ship; they are both inn and trail. We, black women, do both." They had to, of course. Black women, except perhaps in the black upper classes, did not often have the luxury of choosing between marriage and career. (And often, black families became upper class because the wife worked.)

You'll be told you're more emotional than men. Nonsense. It's just that in our society, women are allowed to show their emotions and men are not supposed to show theirs. (Men have cranky cycles just as women do, and men also go through their own menopause.)

It is generally accepted that males are more aggressive than females, and that females are more perceptive than males (this is not true of all males or all females, only on the average). There are two schools of thought about whether males and females are psychosexually different at birth, or only experience and conditioning makes them different. Silly argument. Anyone can be taught a little extra assertiveness or gentled down no matter what the birth sex. And it takes both strength and perception to do the work of the world. Understanding a situation is just as necessary as getting in there and fighting about it.

In most countries of the world, all the important decisions about life are made by men. And the world is a mess. It may be that the talents of both sexes are necessary if we're going to improve things. Certainly women shouldn't complain about the state of the world unless we're willing to shoulder half the responsibility, or maybe unless we're willing to fight to get half the responsibility.

As a Cherokee Indian teenage girl wrote in *Girl Power*, "I can't justify complaining about anything I am not willing to change."

It's true that the working world is difficult for women. Life in general is difficult for people who are sat on. The thing to do is stand up. That way, you remove the lap, and there is no place for anybody to sit. It also leaves the legs free for walking or running wherever you want to go.

Women And The Arts

I n discussions with men on the subject of women's liberation, there are two things I keep hearing over and over from those who are male chauvinists. (A male chauvinist, once known as a pig, is a man who thinks, or behaves as if he thinks, that women are not as good as men. Or he may think of us as equal in importance, but only as long as we keep to women's work — that is, taking care of *him*, *his* house, *his* babies, and *his* interests. He will call this separate-but-equal. Only somehow separate-but-equal never ends up being equal to the ones who are separate.)

What men say most often is, "Laws have been passed giving you job equality. So if you are as good as men are, how come you haven't gotten better pay and better jobs, more fame, more prizes?"

The answer to that one is easy. You know it already. It's called *discrimination*. Once this is explained to them, the macho men seem to accept it as truth, but then their eyes light up with that triumphant superiority we all know so well and dare us to answer the next question.

"If, as you claim, women's brains are just as good as men's brains, how come there is no female Michelangelo? How come there is no female Shakespeare?"

Why is there no female Michelangelo? Why are there no women's names on the lists of greatness in the visual arts? It is a question that makes men feel terribly smug and makes women feel just plain terrible. It is a question that, if you aren't careful, seems to supply its own answer: "because women just don't have it in them to be great artists."

(Don't panic. It isn't the right answer, because it isn't the right question.)

Generally, when men attack with the question, "Why are there no great women artists?" a feminist who is proud of being a woman will scramble around in her mind to come up with a list of well-known woman painters, architects, and sculptors — Berthe Morisot, Angelica Kauffmann, Rosa Bonheur, Betsey Graves Reyneau, Artemisia Gentileschi, Kathe Kollwitz, Norma Sklarek, the first African-American woman architect to earn a fellowship from the American Institute of Architects, Synthia Saint James, Africa-American artist. A proud feminist will try to prove, by using the names of these women, that there is a history of greatness in the visual arts of women, that it has simply been neglected, overlooked. Champions of women's equality also fall into the trap of trying to puff up the achievements of a limited number of women artists. The trouble is, it doesn't work. The sad truth is that no matter how hard we search, we can't come up with many female artists or any as great as Michelangelo or Rembrandt or Picasso. There just haven't been any.

And it doesn't help to think about what might have been. For instance when one looks at the magnificent needlework of the past, often done by nuns, it makes one feel as if real talent was trapped into a sideline. It isn't a matter of "why are there no great women artists." It's a matter of "why haven't women been *allowed* to be great artists!"

Once again, women never stood a chance. Only part of great art is genius. The other two parts are study and encouragement. Think of the stories of great male artists. The young Giotto, a lowly shepherd boy, was discovered drawing pictures of his sheep on a stone by an old, great artist named Cimabue who was so impressed by the drawings that he immediately invited the boy to be his pupil.

If the young Giotto had been a girl, she would have been told to learn to cook instead. In those days, only males were invited to study under the great masters, never females. Only males were allowed to join the European Arts Guilds, never females. (No different in Africa or the Far East, or in Native American or Hispanic cultures, and in the Middle East, women were hardly let out of women's quarters.) Art is only partly instinct and talent. It also takes a tremendous amount of training. Girls might dabble on their own; they were never allowed training by the great artists. Michelangelo, it is said, did more drawing than studying school lessons as a child. For his efforts, he got to study art under the master Ghirlandaio, who taught and encouraged him and said of him finally, "This boy knows more than I do."

If Michelangelo had been a girl, her mother might have said, "You draw nicely, dear. Now wash the shirts, give the baby his dinner, and sweep the kitchen for me, there's a good girl." She would have been given little time to draw, less encouragement, and no training at all.

To be an artist requires, above all, hours to oneself to practice one's profession. Until recently, and even now, women have had to struggle for time. Females were simply never allowed two minutes off from their household duties to accomplish very much of anything. No artist, male or female, ever made it on artistic genius alone. Time to practice; places to study like art academies or master's studios; encouragement by society, one's fellow artists, one's parents — these are all part of what makes greatness out of talent. What is surprising is not that there are no really great women artists in history, but that there are any at all.

By the nineteenth century, a few heroic women managed to get themselves taught and to emerge as painters. All were either daughters of artists or were close to artists who helped them. It took a tremendous amount of courage and rebellion against society (which approved of women only if they were wives and mothers) to choose a career at all, much less a career in the arts, which had for thousands of years in Japan, China, India, Africa, as well as in Europeanized cultures, been reserved for men only.

In the twentieth century, it has been easier to get oneself taught. But it is almost as difficult as ever to find encouragement and serious acceptance if you are a woman. (I have a woman friend who is an artist. She says that when she talks with men artists, they still seem to think that women's only place in art is as an object to paint, or as an inspiration to the artist. My friend says it's time we stopped modeling for pictures instead of painting them, time we stopped inspiring others and started inspiring ourselves.)

While the question about great women composers (there were none we know of in the past — although there are a few doing excellent work now) must be answered in about the same way as the question about great women artists, the history of great women writers is a little different. There is no Wilma Shakespeare, it is true. Women, four hundred years ago, were not even educated except rarely, much less let out of the house to traipse off to London to learn the theater business. If Wilma had managed to learn to read, and was found mooning over books, her mother would have told her to mind the stew and then married her off like a shot. If by some chance Wilma had managed to find her way to London's theaters and asked for a job, the managers would have laughed in her face. No women were allowed even to act (men played the women's roles) much less get enough theater training to write a play.

But if we have produced no playwrights of Shakespeare's stature, we have produced great poets (Emily Dickinson,

Marianne Moore, Maya Angelou) and novelists. Novelists of the last century, Jane Austen, George Eliot, Emily and Charlotte Bronte, Mary Shelley (who wrote *Frankenstein*); of this century, Edith Wharton, Alice Walker, Ann Tyler, Toni Morrison, Virginia Woolf, Eudora Welty, Joyce Carol Oates, Willa Cather, all these of the Western world; and Lady Murasaki of tenth-century Japan (note that a woman produced the first great novel ever written), these are among the women to have written novels equal in artistic greatness to those written by the great male novelists, Dickens, Balzac, Proust, Tolstoy, Dostoyevsky, Faulkner. Women were barred from politics and war, so it is not surprising that no nineteenth-century woman wrote a novel like Tolstoy's *War and Peace*. But on all other aspects of society there is a wealth of brilliant, profound, and passionate literature written by women in the past two hundred years.

Again it must be said that women have had a hard battle for acceptance. The critics were so prejudiced against writers who were women that in the eighteenth century, women published anonymously, and in the nineteenth century, many used masculine names. Charlotte and Emily Bronte used the names Currer and Ellis Bell; George Eliot's name was really Mary Ann Evans. And not only did critics belittle novels if they were known to be written by women, but all of society treated any woman who worked at a profession as if she were a freak. Creativity in women back then was supposed to be confined to arranging flowers and quilting. It was considered immoral for women to take time away from their housework and children to pursue other work unless survival necessitated their labor on farms, in factories, in the fields. (If this kind of gender prejudice seems quaint to you, remember there are still *real* horrors being performed on little girls around the world — genital mutilation in Africa, forced female child prostitution in Thailand and on the streets of North and South American cities, girls drowned or left to die in China, female sweatshops everywhere.)

At least, unlike the other arts, the writing of poetry, essays, and novels was possible for women. It was something that could be done at home and alone. No need, like a painter, to go out in search of an academy, an art school, a model to paint; or like a composer, to have to have musical training. Women at home, even if they were not formally educated at schools like their brothers, could read books for themselves and learn how to write by reading. And then, writing could be dropped at a moment's notice to meet the demands of family life. It might also be added that writing materials are cheap — no need for costly art supplies or instruments.

At least now it is acceptable for women to have literary ambitions, to want to publish and make money from writing good literature. It still isn't easy, though, for women to achieve the discipline and dedication it takes to be a professional in the creative arts. Gifts, brains, and genius are the property of both sexes; but for these to develop there must be encouragement, acceptance, education, and above all, hours and hours and hours of free time. (Think of today's superwomen, who must do most of the housework and childcare as well as work, either as a single head-of-household or as earners in a household requiring two incomes.

The emancipation of women is still spectacularly new after ten thousand years of civilization, and still far from actualized. We have begun to develop as writers, as artists, as composers, even if jazz and blues are still male domains. But emancipation does not result in instant achievement. Geniuses are not born every hour. Even among men, who have had so much more opportunity to develop, the really great are few in number.

How many times have you heard, "Women don't need to be creative. Making babies is the greatest act of creation there is." Making babies is indeed wonderful, and certainly there wouldn't be any life anywhere without that particular form of activity. But making babies is nature's miracle, not the miracle of a single inventive mind. And did you ever hear anybody tell a man that fathering a baby was all he had to do to be creative?

We must beware of saying to ourselves: babies are enough to create, babies are like beautiful pictures, poems, symphonies. Babies are great. But they aren't like pictures, poems, or songs, they are like babies. In the history of human kind, half the geniuses ever born, the half that were women, have died without having been allowed to follow their stars. The future must be different. We can't afford to waste human talent on that scale.

Women's Image In Advertising & What They Do To You At The Mall

O f all the woman-haters that have ever lived, advertisers must rank among the worst. Every time you turn on the television set, the commercials are there to tell you every few minutes, day after day, year after year, that you are an idiot, and a ridiculous idiot at that. You can be seen looking cool, gorgeous, sexy, twitching every female muscle to catch a boyfriend or the attention of a husband; you can be seen on your knees waxing a floor, bending over a stove, cleaning, washing, diapering a baby. Mommies, not daddies, are still putting on the band-aids, doing the laundry, rejoicing over a little boy's thrill over his Pull-Ups, cooing over cereals. And it's mom on the job who gets telephoned in emergencies. Despite her power suit, she's the parent to the rescue, the one who cooks the quickie breakfasts on the way to the office, the household chief-of-staff. And not only do you do double duty as lawyer-mommy, doctor-mommy, physicist-mommy, senator-mommy, servant to the world and your family, but you are *thrilled* to be doing it!

When you are pictured outside the kitchen, you will generally be found as the Happy Helper or Cheerful Cheerleader, secretarying men in offices, serving them on airplanes. Men do these things now, too, but it is women who are mostly pictured this way. Not that it matters to your television self what you are doing, since your major interest in life anyway is what the advertisers call the "male reward." Advertisers snigger over what they feel is a sure bet: that you'll do any kind of work, go through any kind of drudgery, spend any amount of time, money, and agony on push-up bras, clothes, and makeup, crawl, cringe, and scrape — anything, so long as at the end of it, some male pats you on the head like a good girl (dog?).

(If you don't believe it, turn on your TV now and flip around. I just did. Women were cooking, sewing, playing with dolls, selling dolls, dying or treating their hair, and making kissy lips at the camera. There was a woman making her magic vacuum cleaner clean all the way to China. The men in the commercials were driving heavy machinery, surfboarding, and running the world.

(This is what, in our local high school, encourages girls to take Home Economics and Fashion Design instead joining the boys — even where the girls are invited — in architecture and woodwork shop, science workshops, computer labs.

Advertising puts woman in her place as household and office servant and sex object and keeps her there.

Advertising is a terrible propaganda machine for a male supremacist society. It tells both men and women that women are stupid childlike creatures whose main abilities are those of sex partner, housekeeper, baby maker, and home/office/factory servant. And the commercials run so often, and they are seen by so many millions of people that, like the Chinese water torture, the drops of poison go on dripping until everybody is convinced that there must be some truth to the commercial images. On and on goes the same image: men run the world; and women are only fit to amuse and serve the men. It's humiliating, degrading, and disgusting.

There are 103 million women in the U.S. over 16. Among adult women, 59% were in the labor force in 1995; among teenage women 16-19, 52%. Half the students in law and medical school are women. Yet men still think of successful women as fake men in skirts. (And we still haven't shattered that glass ceiling. In 1970, the top managers of major American corporations were 99% male; almost 30 years later, it's still 95%. The percentage of high-level women seems stuck at under 10% — even in Congress, women were 6% of elected representatives in the 1990's, up only 2% from the 1950's.)

Women don't love this. It exhausts them having to work harder than men, with their responsibilities in as well as outside the house. But if you are portrayed as a dimwit, and perceived as a dimwit, you'll be treated and paid like one.

Sexist advertising begins at a very early age to show girls how silly and unimportant they are. Think of the toys that are advertised on television. The boys are shown creating things with blocks or learning with science kits. But for the girls there are still mostly Barbie dolls so they learn young what they are supposed to do when they grow up: wear cool clothes and attract men! What this kind of thing produces is a whole generation of girls who will grow up to be forty-five-year-old Barbie dolls. There are Creme Rinse for Children commercials. Children? Have you ever seen a boy in that commercial? Never. While boys jump through mud puddles (so their mothers can wash their clothes three times a day with Crax or Toad or whatever-kind-of-soap it is), a little blond girl with or without her African-American, Hispanic-American, Asian-American, Native-American friends simpers and lisps and pats her hair. It's enough to make you want to slap, not her, but the sponsor.

When the commercial-advertisement girl gets too old for dolls, her only interested in life becomes boys — not herself or the world or the work she will do. According to television, a girl's only activity is to get a boy, any boy, quick.

If you take the advice of television commercials or magazine ads, you will grin insanely at him with ultra bright toothpaste on your teeth; you will suck a breath mint in his face so he will kiss you; you will use a lover-friendly mouthwash (or presumably you won't have a friendly lover); you will drink diet drinks until you're so skinny he won't be able to see you if you turn sideways; you will get whiter or tanner, buy some more hair, shorten and tighten your skirts, pump up your muscles, tattoo and pierce your ears, nose, lips, eyebrows, and bellybuttons until you faint from the pain and the infections. (While you're doing all this, you'd better cross your fingers that he hasn't gone off with some girl who's got more interesting things on her mind.)

Not that television and magazine people really think any of you has a mind. I remember an ad for a famous pen. "You might as well give her a gorgeous pen to keep her checkbook unbalanced with. A sleek and shining pen will make her feel prettier. Which is more important to any girl than solving mathematical mysteries."

And then when you've finally done the one thing everybody wanted you to do and gotten married, are you at long last given the respect due to any human being? Don't be funny. Now you have really become an absurd joke to the media. Listen to the married moms in commercials actually singing about their detergents, dancing around the house with their bleaches. (Can you imagine what their husbands would do if they came home and really found their wives dancing and shrieking over their supermarket products?)

You'd think, watching commercials, that youthful housewives, who are constantly pictured surrounded by washing machines, dryers, ovens, blenders, coffee pots, microwaves, standing on newly tiled, freshly waxed floors, talking about their laundry, the cooking, have nothing else of much importance on their minds. It's a joke. But it's a sad joke. Because while it's all made to seem meaningful, the reality is that the world thinks so little of housework and gives it so little status, that domestic work is about the lowest-paying job you can get. The ads fool you into thinking how much satisfaction you'll get from a dish you can see your face in. But the fact remains, there is simply nothing very challenging about everyday cleaning. The ads play on the fact that many women are afraid to admit they don't like housework, that they'll be thought unfeminine. Advertisers are playing on that psychological fear very cruelly.

The main thing these ads and commercials accomplish is to make women feel their chief role in life is to please men, serve their families, and stay in the kitchen as much as possible. Commercials may show them driving Jeeps and throwing Frisbees across mountain tops and playing basketball and directing board meetings or brain surgeries, but if you look for it, the female rather than the plain human angle is usually apparent. Not only does this reinforce men's views of a woman's place in the home, kitchen, or bed, but it all pictures us as a race of not-very-bright children. Since more women graduated from high school and enrolled in college in 1995 than men, it is both an insult and an outrage that we are still being shown to the world as if we had all been dropped on our heads.

Even in commercials geared to men, how often do you see a woman attracted or given away as a trophy just because he buys a car or a drink? And while now and then, women are shown in enough possession of their faculties to buy themselves a car or a piece of jewelry, it is more often the men who are persuaded to buy them bigger and better goodies. (It is a fallacy that women control the purse strings of the nation. They may do all the shopping, but it's for laundry soap, not for college education, life insurance, investments, or cars.)

Speaking of bigger-and-better-or-just-newer goodies, there is another way society takes advantage of lonely and frustrated girls, women, wives. Women's magazines, television, and mall stores are all trying to con women into thinking they will find fulfillment in buying more 'things' — especially if those 'things' are either for home-and-family or to make her look more fascinating to her husband or boyfriend (clothes, cosmetics). If a woman can be brainwashed (and after so much hammering on the head, many women can't help but be) into feeling that her whole life can be changed by a new shower curtain or a new pair of eyelashes, mall store sales go up and up and up.

Malls play with your mind in another way, too. Since many women live lonely lives within the walls of their houses and fear that life is passing them by, stores offer women an experience, a lesson, in what's going on in the world of new products, new discoveries, new fashions. They make women feel more in touch with the outside world. They also make a woman feel she is an expert in something, even if it's only the right polish to use, the newest thing in exercise equipment, the latest in quilts and refrigerators.

Bargain sales are another way stores cheat women. They have managed to make a woman feel virtuous, like a good little homemaker, if she buys something on sale, especially in a discount store. A sale price makes her think, "I'm doing a good job as a housewife. I'm contributing to the welfare of my family in the same way my husband does when he brings home a paycheck." The sad part is, she will buy anything, even if she doesn't need it, just to have that virtuous feeling.

But remember, the commercials and ads and store windows are only mirrors. It is society that creates the narrow roles in the first place. And maybe these mirrors can teach us a lesson. If, as girls and women, we look long enough and hard enough at those humiliating mirrors, it might make a lot of us realize how sad our condition is if our only goals in life are cleaner floors, leakless diapers, or a new lipstick that won't kiss off.

That stuff is all right in its place, but it's not enough. And if you doubt it, just switch the image to a man. Would it be enough for a man to have the cleanest floors in the neighborhood? To have the prettiest skin?

Well, if it isn't enough for him, then it isn't enough for you!

There's Something Wrong With Your Rights

Did you know that nowhere in the Constitution of the United States does it state that women are citizens? Women have never been legally declared persons in this country, not by the Founding Fathers (there were, naturally, no Founding Mothers), not by the Constitution, not by the Supreme Court. The Fifteenth Amendment guarantees the right to vote to all U.S. citizens, whatever their color or race and whether they had been born free or born slaves, but this did not include women.

Women fought for the abolition of slavery. When the battle was won, black men got the vote. Black women did not. Nor white women either.

To win the vote, women ran 56 referendum campaigns; 804 campaigns in the states; 19 campaigns in 19 consecutive Congresses. The effort to win our right to vote took 52 years, until in 1920, the Nineteenth Amendment was passed.

Those regions of the country that were most racist were also the most antifeminist. Of the ten states that refused to agree to the Nineteenth Amendment, nine were southern. The tenth was Delaware. The white male looked down on blacks and women alike. Even Thomas Jefferson said that women, slaves, and babies should be kept away from political decisions. (And there's a big monument built to him!)

The region where women fared best was the West, where they had fought and pioneered alongside their men. Wyoming refused to become a state and join the Union unless its women, who had already been given voting rights within the territory, could keep those rights. "We will remain out of the Union a hundred years rather than come in without the women," they said.

But even though we finally got the right to vote, women still have very little actual political power. This is partly due to male discrimination against women, to their feeling that women are not intellectually capable of making important political decisions or that women are too emotionally unstable to be trusted with the affairs of the nation. It is also partly due to the fact that many women, themselves, believe this to be true and would not run for office or vote for women.

This is partly based on our so-called family values that insists the only way to bring children up is in an American nuclear unit — despite the fact that children all over the world are successfully reared in extended, many-generational systems. The importance of women's votes, however, is very clear: they have been known to swing entire presidential elections! And as for their political presence — many educational and environmental issues would be lost without women.

Only a handful of women have been elected to the Senate and Congress of the United States. There are only a token number of women federal judges, although we finally have two women Justices of the Supreme Court and a woman Attorney General, Janet Reno. There are few women governors or mayors.

In many countries all over the world, women are worse off. But even in the United States, after a 10-year battle, there was the failure to ratify the Equal Rights Amendment in 1982. There has been the denaturing of affirmative action laws. Terrorism like the bombing of abortion clinics continues to follow the important Roe v Wade decision in which the Supreme Court ruled 7-2 that a state may not prevent a woman from having an abortion during the first three months of pregnancy. Women are watching their rights slip away even in the United States.

In other parts of the Planet Earth, women have few rights at all. In Zaire and Bosnia, women were recently raped by the thousands by males of conquering tribes not only as an act of war, but to ensure the seed of the conquering tribes.

The rapists have not been tried for war crimes. Only recently has Japan grudgingly apologized for forcibly confining women in "comfort stations" (houses of prostitution) during WWII to service Japanese troops. Fundamentalist Islamic mullahs keep Islamic women in the veil and without political power or even basic human rights.

There was the United Nations Declaration of Human Rights, the UN World Conference on Women in 1985, the 1994 Cairo Third International Conference on Population and Development. There was the Bill of Rights for Women hammered out at Beijing in 1995 (present were 30,000 women strong, from Finland to India, from Ecuador to New Guinea to Mongolia, prime ministers and village midwives, Nobel Prize winners and wildlife rehabilitators).

But despite all this there has been very little worldwide progress in the common problems of girls and women. These are poverty, gender equality in education, health care, the violence committed against them, and their general lack of political power, whether that is in relationship to their husbands, fathers, and sons or their countries or the United Nations itself.

There was a woman from Bangladesh at the Beijing Conference who discovered that she was more like her husband than his cattle. An Indian woman refused to leave her daughter to die. A Thai woman decided not to sell herself or her daughter into prostitution to pay her family's debts. China has taken great pride in freeing its women from household bondage and providing day-care centers for children so the women are able to work — but it's still the men who run the government, and the Chinese women were angry.

In a 1995 Geneva study, it was found that the percentage of women elected to national legislatures worldwide has dropped by nearly a quarter since the collapse of communism in Europe and since the free elections in Africa. The odd exception in South Asia in the 1980's and the 1990's when wives and daughters of former political leaders became heads of government in countries where women were most oppressed — India, Pakistan, Bangladesh, Sri Lanka — had nothing to do with equality. It was simply medievalism — a woman from a top caste family was superior to other men. The fury of a woman from sub-Saharan Africa (along with rural China and India, parts of Latin America, Outback Australia, and the Philippines, one of the poorest countries in the world) was quoted in the media: "We continue to be second-rate citizens — no, third-rate, since our sons come before us and even donkeys and tractors get better treatment."

Our sisters all over the world suffer. In certain African countries, women are still holding down two million of their daughters each year so that their tiny genitalia can be mutilated in the name of marketability and chastity in the marriage market. In the Philippines, sex tourism enslaves children and adolescents in brothels; in China and India, female infanticide is rising. In 1992 a Dutch study of the international sex trade had warned that "European merchants had begun to exploit the last natural resource of the Third World — its women." These women were promised jobs as domestic workers and were forced into sexual slavery. In 1990, three thousand women were in jail in Pakistan, the result of laws of the religious fundamentalists that made it a criminal act for women to file for divorce or report a rape.

Make no mistake. In our own country, too, terrorism against women, bombing women's clinics, stalking (on the Internet as well as on the streets) and rape, child abuses, incest, sexual harassment that remains unprosecuted, is increasing. Fanatic religious fundamentalism, meaning male-dominated religious groups that want to keep women at home to be sex and household servants with men in power over them, exists in the United States as well.

Without power, we cannot help make or change the laws. We may lobby, campaign, fight, and vote, but we must run for office if we truly want to be in a position to make changes in the laws that are unfair to women. "Make policy, not coffee," was the motto of one Women's Political Caucus.

Because there are still many unfair laws.

There was once a debate in the legislature of Tennessee. It was stated at the time that women had no souls — therefore, the law would not permit them to own property.

Many of our problems with the laws in this country began when we were not declared citizens, continued when we were refused the vote, and are still aggravated because we do not have very much political power. Among the worst of these problems are the laws for married women about MONEY.

Although most married women in this country work outside the home, many women are housewives. A housewife means you work up to fourteen or more hours a day as nursemaid, dietitian, food buyer, chauffeur, dishwasher, housekeeper, launderer, practical nurse, maintenance person, gardener, and cook — for nothing. No salary, no insurance, no Social Security, no pension plan. Food, clothing, and shelter are generally provided. Anything else you get depends on the good nature of your husband. And you have to *ask* for it. You have no *right* to it.

In all but a few states, a husband's earnings are his separate, personal property. His wife has no legal claim on his money or on any property in his name. Even in the few states where there is a thing called community property laws and everything is supposedly owned by both husband and wife, the property is still under the husband's sole control if he bought it.

What this means is that housewives can work their whole lives long and never have the lawful right to one red cent!

A woman I know not only did the household chores for her family and brought up the children, but on top of that helped her husband by working in his florist shop many hours every day. After twenty years, she wanted to leave him. But after all those years of work, both inside and outside the home, she still had no right to any money. She cannot claim back salary because she was working for her husband; she cannot claim a share of the business, because, that, of course, belongs to him solely since it is in his name. She is out of luck altogether.

When there is a divorce, people are always talking about how unfair it is to the man to have to pay alimony. There is always the picture of men working hard, and divorced women just sitting around eating boxes of chocolate after their face lifts and weeks on a cruise. The facts are quite different. Although by law, the husband must pay for child support, many women either don't get alimony, or get such a low amount they can barely manage. And this, after the wife has worked for the husband for nothing as a housekeeper for all the years they were married. Most women think of alimony, not as a charity gift, but as back pay for the work they did. According to some economists, housewives are doing free work worth at least $400 a week on the current labor market.

When people make fun of a housewife's work, it is only because it is a *woman* who is doing it. Men who cook are chefs; women who cook are just cooks. Men who handle finances are accountants; women are often still called just bookkeepers even if they have a CPA degree. In the 1970's, the Labor Department's *Dictionary of Occupational Titles*, which grades 22,000 occupations on a skill scale from a high of 1 to a low of 887, rates homemakers near the bottom at 876 (along with foster mothers, nursery school teachers, and practical nurses). Not much has changed in public opinion.

Even women downgrade themselves by saying, "I don't work, I'm just a housewife." Now there are lots of people, men as well as women, who are happier working at home than working in the outside world. With the new computer technology, many men are opting to work at home, as do artists of both sexes and many self-employed people. Staying at home should be allowed to men as well as to women. And what's wrong with a woman working at an outside job to support her husband, if he's the one who prefers the housekeeping?

But when it is the woman who stays home, and since she is the one whose rights to money is the problem, the laws must be changed so that she is paid in some way, legally, for her work. Getting love for what you do is wonderful, but if there's trouble, you can't live on love. Either, 1) housewives should be paid a salary by their husbands (or some part of his income should be hers by law); 2) there should be a law to make sure that if the marriage ends, she is paid back salary; or 3) housework should be placed in the category of jobs covered by the Social Security system, so that she contribute accordingly and can collect money as other workers do after retirement. The business of simply relegating childcare automatically to women as their business is absurd. Think about it. Don't children belong to everybody? And if you're thinking in terms of numbers, actually, women can only have one child a year for a limited period of years. Men can father children all the time, almost all their lives!

The point of all this is to be practical. Women can choose their careers. Whether they work in the home or outside the home, they should be paid, legally, for the work they do.

Juvenile delinquency laws are unfair to girls in many states. Until recently, under New York's Family Court Act, a boy who ran away from home (without just cause) after the age of sixteen would not have been returned to his home. A girl would have been returned to her home until she was eighteen.

There were two teenagers in Westchester, New York; a boy, seventeen, and a girl, seventeen. The parents of both teenagers brought them to court because both stayed out too late at night, both hung around with undesirable companions, and both had contracted a venereal disease. The girl, because she was under eighteen, was declared by the court to be a "Person in Need of Supervision," and she was sent to a state training school for rehabilitation. The boy was let go. "Boys will be boys," said the judge.

There are some acts that are crimes only if they are done by women. In convictions of prostitution, it is the girls and women who are jailed or fined or both. As for the boys and men who engage the prostitutes, well, boys will be boys, says the judicial system, and they are let go. Very few localities, though there are a few, publish the names of the "johns" after they are arrested.

Two other areas of discrimination against women are housing and credit. In many places, single women find it difficult to rent a house or an apartment, even if they have perfectly good jobs and can well afford the rent. The grounds for the landlord's discrimination is that women, like children, can't be trusted to pay their bills. Women who are divorced have special troubles. In New York City, a recently divorced woman with a young child had difficult getting an apartment because the landlords kept insisting "that all divorced women give noisy parties and never pay their rent on time." What made this particular story doubly idiotic was that a quieter, more sedate woman never lived!

In some areas of the United States a single woman may have trouble getting credit to make large purchases. She will have to get a male relative to co-sign if she wants to buy a home or if she wants credit for another large purchase. I know of one woman who had been the sole support of her family for ten years. Her husband had been seriously ill and hadn't been able to work. But despite this, when the time came to buy a house, the papers had to be signed by him! One study showed that women, especially black women, paid higher prices for cars when negotiation was necessary.

Thousands of women all over the country have organized to fight for the rights of women under the law. In the United States, the slow pace of electoral change drove women to create their own political organizations in the 1980's, such as EMILY'S List. Separate from male-dominated party organizations, this fund-raising group supported and helped to elect more women to office in federal and state elections from 1992 on. Women in India got a law passed in the 1990's mandating that 33% of elective positions be reserved for women. Women's small banks and loan societies were launched around the world for poor women to borrow small start-up

funds for self-employment, cottage industries, an idea begun by the Women's World Bank in the 1970's.

In the United States, the Equal Rights Amendment was
passed by Congress in March 1972. This amendment would
forbid discrimination based on sex by any law or action of
federal, state, or local government. The amendment was
NOT ratified by the states ten years later..

The powers of the Equal Employment Opportunity Commission to enforce nondiscrimination in employment must
be strengthened. The Equal Pay Act must be strengthened
and enforced, so that professional, administrative, and executive women will get the same pay and the same promotions as men for the same work.

Under Title IX of the Education Amendments of 1972,
discrimination on the basis of sex became illegal in an
education program receiving federal funding. But the U.S.
Office of Civil Rights has not enforced this. There were
reports quoted that it was "stupid" or "frivolous" to worry
about equal opportunities for girls and for boys. It must be
said once more that it takes more than a change of laws to
change attitudes.

New rules of the Equal Employment Opportunity Commission give more rights to pregnant women employees. The
Civil Rights Act of 1964 makes it illegal to deny a woman a
job because she is pregnant, and women who take maternity leave must be given sick pay.

Women are also still fighting for the right to their own
bodies, the rights to make their own decisions about whether
they want to bear children or not. All over the world, women

are refusing to have unwanted children — upwards of 50 million abortions are reportedly performed each year. But until recently they've had to duck male-made laws against abortions, and often had to go to quacks. There is so much backlash against the Roe vs. Wade decision, that we are in danger of being pushed back to the days when you could get an abortion if the doctors agreed that having a baby would injure your health. In Italy and Mexico, abortions are illegal, but they are cheap and easy to get. In Bulgaria, Hungary, Japan, Scandinavia, Russia, China, abortion is legal. Conditions differ everywhere (and the laws, as in Poland, keep changing), but in very few places have women had the right to decide for themselves whether they want or do not want to remain pregnant. Feminists feel that just as women who are against abortion should have a right to their opinion, women who believe in abortion should have a right to have one if they want.

Another very important fight is for improvement in the number and quality of day-care centers, so that mothers who want to work have clean, well-staffed places to leave their children during working hours. These day-care centers should either be free or be inexpensive enough so that working people can afford them easily.

The time has come (actually, it came a long time ago, but women don't seem to have talked to each other and banded together to do something about their common problems until recently) when politics and lawmaking can no longer be left solely in the hands of men. We must help and protect ourselves — housewives, workers, professional women, teenage girls — with equal education, equal laws, equal pay for equal work, equal job opportunities. We must fight for day-care systems and the right to control our own bodies. We must have a system in place to protect us against battering and domestic violence. We must have enough power to ensure a voice in the affairs of the nation, whether the affairs are women's issues or poverty or racism or war. It isn't easy to break the male prejudice barrier, or the anger of women in the traditional roles of wife/mother. As Shirley Chisholm, New York Congresswoman and 1972 candidate for the presidency of the United States, once said, "As a black person, I am no stranger to race prejudice. But the truth is that in the political world I have been far oftener discriminated against because I am a woman than because I am black."

A Latina high school girl, a Riot Grrrl, I know said, "We have to stop using quick fixes — pregnancy, drugs, overeating — against sexism and empower ourselves instead of hating ourselves like everybody else does."

She's right. We've got to fight — fight and shout and scream and holler, if that's what it takes. And if that ruins our image as sweet little ladylike darlings — well, where did being sweet little ladylike darlings get us anyway, except into a television commercial behind a dishpan!

The Beautiful Imbecile

Do you look like a supermodel, an MTV rockstar, a moviestar, a California bleached, baked, bony, beachbunny, or Miss Teenage America? Do you have long legs, long eyelashes, a small waist, a big bust, narrow hips, large eyes, a good butt, shining hair, a perfect smile, and a sexy walk? Are you at least pierced, pouty-lipped, picturesque with tattoos?

No? Shoot yourself.

You might as well get it over with now as spend the rest of your life in the agony most women go through with their looks, the agony of the beauty game. It's a game you're forced to play from the moment you are born until the day you die, and if for a little while you forget to play, there is always somebody around to remind you. A girlfriend, your boyfriend, your mother, salespeople in a commercial — somebody is always there to suggest you're too fat or too short, you need a pushier bra, you need a cream rinse or a wig, a new eyeliner, face cream, or lipstick, a shorter skirt or longer nails or a nose-ring. Whatever it is, you need something, because you're certainly not all right the way you are.

It's a terrible game, because there's no way you can win. For one thing, the rules keep changing, so even if you look all right now, wait ten minutes and you'll be out of style again. And then, even if you happen to be the rarest of beauties, one day the wrinkles and the gray hair will come, to depress you for the rest of your life or plunge you into the next stage of the game — facelifts, stomach-staples, liposuction — so you can go on being an insecure teenager forever.

It's infuriating, the way we've been made miserable over our looks, the way we've been pushed into such a frantic pursuit of beauty.

Of course, it's hardly surprising. Even before a baby is born, parents sit around crossing their fingers and hoping that if it's a girl she'll be pretty. When she's born, they inspect closely. If she's pretty, there's a general sight of relief. But even if she's a dud in the looks department, they'll say, "maybe she'll be pretty when she grows up," or "at least she'll have a pretty figure," or "well, we'll dress her in pretty clothes."

Pretty, pretty, pretty. Does it matter if she has talent or brains? Not on your life!

And as a little girls grows up, what does she see around her? She sees her mother trying to be pretty for her father or someone else. She sees ads in magazines, commercials on television, fashion on the Internet, all telling her that a girl had better be pretty or she'll never get a man. In movies, it's always the pretty girl who is loved (the other girl is the 'best friend'). Wherever she looks, there are beautiful female media images, on book and CD covers, on billboards on the highways, on MTV. It can't help but make her think that if a woman isn't pretty, she's hardly a woman at all.

As she grows up, people are always harping on her appearance. Don't get your pretty dress dirty. Can't you wear something prettier than those jeans? Why don't you comb your hair so you'll look prettier? Is that girl a dog or what? Is it any wonder that by the time a girl is in her teens, she holds the secret belief that it is more important to be pretty than to be anything else in the world? Society has made such a big deal about beauty that most girls, given the choice, would pick beauty instead of brains. They would rather look like Miss Universe than win the Nobel Prize for chemistry like Dorothy Crowfoot Hodgkin did, who not only discovered the structures of penicillin and vitamin B12, but the biochemical compounds to combat pernicious anemia. They would rather become a supermodel than write novels that rank among the world's greatest literature like Emily Bronte and Lady Murasaki.

Speaking of such choices, an interesting point should be made about two female novelists. As great as she was, George Eliot agonized all her life over not being pretty. So did Charlotte Bronte, Emily's sister. Great male writers like Dante and Emerson were ugly, too, but nobody ever bothered them about it, nor did they bother themselves. Critics harp on whether great women are pretty because they would rather think of them as women than as great minds. Hillary Rodham Clinton, author of *It Takes a Village (To Raise a Child)*, lawyer, First Lady, has sold more books than her husband the President, but appears nowhere without every hair in place. When you see a story about an important woman executive or read that a woman has gained a political position, how often have you read "And she is pretty, too?" Do they ever comment on how handsome a male judge is or on the hairdo of a male executive? Just once I'd like to read, "George Smithers, hair curled enchantingly over his ears, dressed in a divine double-breasted, London-tailored suit, has just been elected Governor of...."

What women have gone through to be beautiful has often been painful and is almost always uncomfortable. For centuries the women of China bound their feet because the ideal foot was tiny. Binding the feet tightly was excruciating for little girls. It made bones break, toes drop off, and often gangrene set in, bringing death. A thousand years ago in Japan, women who wanted to be fashionable had to paint their teeth black and wear their hair so long they could hardly stand up under the weight of it, much less get around the palace. In tribal societies where it is fashionable to be fat, women force-feed themselves like geese. In many societies, including ours today, girls have gone through the pain of piercing sensitive tissues. Women undergo surgery to have their faces smoothed, their skin peeled, their breasts filled out, their noses and thighs reshaped. They starve. They endure the pain of electrolysis to rid their bodies of hair. They endure numbness in their breasts to have implants.

Simply, what women do to be pretty is go through hell. And even if you decide not to torture yourself about the way you look, the rest of the world will remind you daily whether you are attractive or not.

The Pain of Beauty

A famous Somalian supermodel, in an interview with Barbara Walters on 20/20, tells one of the most terrible stories of all. She was held down by her mother, as all five-year-old girls were in her tribe, to have her clitoris cut out and her vagina sewn closed. Unless she died from a carelessly cut vein or infection (many girls do die from this) she became the property of a husband. After marriage, each time there was sex or a baby, she would have to be cut open and sewn up again to ensure her chastity and fidelity. When the beautiful girl asked her father why, she was told a man would no more leave his woman open to thieves than the door of his house.

The beautiful model said that a hundred million women are butchered this way. She herself, at thirteen, to escape marriage to an old man chosen by her father in exchange for two camels, ran away, walking two hundred miles, wrapped only in a cloth, to Mogadishu. Relatives got her to London. She tells her painful secret as part of her fight to save little girls from such butchery as she suffered. As Pamela McCorduck and Nancy Ramsey point out in their book *The Futures of Women*, television and computer technology will soon allow all women to see how some women live, and this information technology will help to revolutionize life for girls everywhere.

The reason for the beauty game, and the mutilations, is that girls are rarely brought up to be fully developed human beings. We are not brought up to be work companions or mental companions for men, but primarily sexual companions. Like animals, we are supposed to use our bodies, but not our minds, in the marriage market. We are told from the beginning that men like their women beautiful and fertile, not bright. When Martin Luther spoke of women, he said, "No dress or garment is less becoming to a woman than a show of intelligence." And girls today are still being told never to let a man find out how smart they are — unless, of course, they are so gorgeous no one will listen to them anyhow, on the theory that if you're all that beautiful, you can't possibly have a brain in your head.

Unfortunately, women have been brought up to feel the same way men feel. Just as men expect women to be beautiful, women expect it of themselves. If a woman is intelligent, if she goes ahead, in spite of everybody's disapproval, and gets herself a college education, a degree, an interesting or intellectual job, she very often worries whether she has become unsexy because of it. That's why so many women doctors, professors, executives, writers will wear a frilly blouse or have their hair teased or show their legs under a short skirt — to reassure themselves and the people they meet that even though they're smart, they're still sexy.

The short skirt and the teeny-weeny bikini (a famous woman doctor I know said to a friend, "Come join me on the beach. I'll be the one wearing the dental floss") deserve mention here. Girls hear older people say that young women today are more sexually liberated than ever before, and if you don't believe it, look at the clothes. This just isn't true. Women may enjoy wearing looser, easier to wear clothes, pants, sweaters. But the revealing clothes and the publicized promiscuity don't express our sexuality, they express our desire to please men as we were brought up to do. In the Victorian age, as in the female-veiled fundamentalist Islamic communities today, men preferred their women to look innocent and hidden, so women wore skirts down to the floor and buttons up to their chins. Then Western men got bored with the innocent look, and they now want us to look sexy.

But you're still only supposed to look that way, not act that way. No, the new clothes and the flinging around of half-naked bodies are not the result of *our sexual freedom. They reflect more than ever the fact that we are still sexual objects for men.* If you don't believe this, listen to how often everybody calls you a slut on the slightest provocation of your reputation. They call boys a *stud* for the same behavior, but in their case, it's a compliment.

In the past, men fussed over their appearances as much as women. Among the Greeks, the ideal beauty was male; among many native tribes everywhere, it's the men who wear the beads and feathers; in the great courts of the East and the West, men wore nearly as many frills, perfumes, and wigs as women did, but around the 1830's, Western men seem to have gotten bored or too busy to keep up elaborate appearances and gave up bright clothes, jewelry, and hair-pieces for simple, comfortable suits and short, unset hair. The whole burden of beauty was shifted to us, and it's just too much for one sex to have to bear. Let them go back to being nervous about the shape of their legs and the drape of their clothes, and give us time to think about the future of humanity and the universe for a change.

But aside from the pain, the burden, and bother, a lot of psychological damage is caused by this business of only the lovely are loved.

If you're not lovely, you get the feeling no one will ever love you.

If you are lovely, you get the feeling that what you are as a person doesn't matter, that men want you only because you have a pretty face or figure, skin tone or hair length and texture.

If you are lovely or if you are not lovely, you will fear getting older, because American/European society tells you (such nonsense!) all there is to life is youth and being pretty.

And you spend all of your life depending like a child on other people's opinion of you, instead of your opinion of yourself. You don't enjoy your accomplishments as a man does; your pride is centered in your physical being. A man is judged by the work he does. If he does not work, the choice is (usually) his. But the world judges you by your face. And if it isn't pretty, there's nothing much you can do about it. If you are pretty, it can be just as disastrous. An exceptionally pretty, young friend of mine, watching her daughter play on the beach, said, "I hope she doesn't grow up as beautiful as she is now. My own mother said to me when I was accepted for college, 'Don't waste your father's money. You're too pretty to be college material. Get a man. Get married.'"

It's too bad that our society discourages girls from reaching for a glory that lasts and encourages them instead to reach for beauty — which doesn't last. And the beauty game is a piece of insanity anyway, because the truth is that men are just as beautiful as women.

There's no reason not to be attractive and enjoy an appreciative glance from a man. There's no reason why a man shouldn't be attractive and enjoy an appreciative glance from a woman. But the duty of having to be the "beautiful" sex, the silliness of having to hide our intelligence behind sexy clothes, and the childishness of having to depend on other people for our sense of worth is a sad and often tragic business.

Men may prefer to keep women in the position of pretty idiots, but women are beginning to prefer not to be kept in that position.

The Happy Housewife

All across America, millions of women make the beds, shop for groceries, do the family wash, chauffeur their children, cook the dinner, sew their husbands' buttons, and they do it all whether they work or not and whether they like it or not. What's more, they're supposed to do it with a smile, because, as John Stuart Mill said in 1860, "All men…desire to have, in the woman most nearly connected with them, not a forced slave but a willing one."

Or, as a male neighbor of mine put it only yesterday, while he was watching his granddaughter swinging expertly on the monkey bars, "What a tomboy! Always out there. Just like my daughter, her mother."

"May she remain so," I said fervently.

"Oh no," said the man. "I like my women at home. They are so much better at nurturing than men are."

Flattery, as well as force, is an excellent method for making life a prison for women.

Learning to salute the master starts young.

Remember? You're to understand his interests come first, you do what he wants to do, go where he goes. You learn not to win the tennis match (high school debate, better grades, and when you get older, higher salaries, job promotions, political arguments) against him — ever. It's natural for him to win, of course. He's been brought up to win. But if you do it, if you win or accomplish anything worthwhile, you've had it. Winning may make the human part of you feel cool, but the *feminine* part of you, the part of you that's been trained to play the female role, ends up feeling like some kind of freak. The boys look at you as if you're strange and, sadly, so do many girls. A good woman slave is supposed to follow her master, not beat him to the draw. (What's awful is that every time you give up or lose on purpose you betray yourself, you lose a little more self-respect and respect for all other women. Losers end up hating themselves and other losers.) But no matter what names you call yourself for giving in all the time, you go on doing it. After all, you've been programmed like a computer to do it.

So why should anything change when you get married? While it's true that you hear now and then of a man who moves for his wife's job transfer or does a long commute for her, for the most part, it's the other way around. You've been brought up to please a man, to do what he wants. And what a man generally wants is somebody else to wash his socks for him.

He doesn't want you to win the rewards the world has to offer; *he* is your reward. He doesn't want you to earn real money (enough to help the family budget is okay); he wants to control the money and the power money brings. He doesn't want you to have the pleasure of standing on your own two feet and feeling like a competent adult; he wants you to stand on his feet so he can choose the direction for both of you to walk. He doesn't want an equal, he wants a worshipper.

The bait for the master-slave trap is that he will take care of you. But why does he have to? You're not mentally impaired or a child, but you are often brought up to believe you are both. So when the great, big man comes along and says he will take care of you, you give up your life, your career, your sense of satisfaction in yourself, and slide gratefully into his arms with a sigh of relief. You will congratulate yourself on your traditional position of wife and mother.

If you're lucky, maybe he will turn out to be strong like your daddy was (or like the imagined father you never had), and gentle and loving like your mommy was (or the one you wish you had), and you can spend the rest of your life snuggling in his arms like a baby. (What you may not find out until afterward, is that, like many men, he is simply an overgrown baby boy, as many girls are overgrown baby girls, and you may be the one who has to come up with the unexpected strength.)

And then, of course, for the first ten years or so of your marriage, you may be so busy with babies that you won't have time to think about much of anything.

Not until the babies grow up and go off to school will there be plenty of time to think. Then there will be empty hour after empty hour after empty hour of time.

Then it may at last occur to you that as wonderful as your husband may be, there is one thing nobody can take care of for someone else. And that is, the sense of one's own worth. The meaning of one's own life. The relationship of one's own life to the rest of life on earth, to god, to the universe.

How often have you heard women say, "I am proud to be a housewife, I am happy being a housewife, I think woman's true role in life is to be a housewife?"

It is true that some people, both men and women, are happy devoting their lives to housekeeping and child care. But that the housewife/mother role is not enough for most women is proved by the many mental health surveys that have been done. The inferior role given to women in marriage has its effect. Overall, more married than single women are reported to be passive, phobic (afraid of things), and depressed. Almost three times as many married as single women show severe symptoms of psychological distress. Many more married women are in psychotherapy than men. Many more women report their marriages as unhappy than men. Twice as many married women as married men have felt they were going to break down. Many more women than men experience psychological and physical anxiety.

Men often say that the reason for women's psychological problems is that women are more emotionally unstable than men, that we are somehow just "crazier" than they are. This is ridiculous. Any group of people that has suffered oppression, prejudice, discrimination, that has been made to feel mentally inferior and physically afraid, that is not allowed to succeed, that is not allowed the satisfaction of full participation in the world's affairs, that is hardly even permitted to win an argument — is going to suffer psychologically for it. Unfair treatment makes the spirit rebel — and if there is no way it can strike back at the world, it will turn the anger inward. And that's what sadness and depression usually are — simply anger at the world turned against the self. Women are, therefore, no more unstable than men; they're just treated worse.

Why do so many women say they are happy, then, to be somebody's wife and somebody's mother, but never somebody themselves? How does a girl who has been a fast runner, a good math student, someone who draws well or writes well or who has engineering talent or dreams of becoming a dancer or a doctor or an editor — how does such a girl suddenly turn into a woman who is deliriously thrilled to be stuck with the dishes, the laundry, and the company of nothing but an undersized population all day? (I know bringing up children is an important job. But it takes two people to make a child, so why should the whole responsibility for care always be a woman's?)

The reason women take all this on and then declare themselves happy to boot is that we have been taught to believe that this is what society expects from us. For some people there is a certain satisfaction in doing, not what they want, but what is expected of them, what they are told is their duty. Sadly, our parents teach us what they were taught — to fit into our sexist, racist, class-conscious, poverty-indifferent, warring society, instead of to live rightly and help save this poor old suffering world. Instead, we do as we have been conditioned to do, and when everybody nods, we interpret this as happiness.

Listening to women who call themselves "happy housewives" is oftentimes a little like watching caged birds whose wings have been clipped. Some women do like it, or adjust to it, but many go on making heartbreaking attempts to fly all their lives. As Maya Angelou, poet, black activist, feminist, wrote: *I Know Why the Caged Bird Sings*.

In the past, when there were no other roads a woman could take, there was some defense for trying to accept things as they were and adjusting to the role of housewife. Healthy people do bow to the unchangeable. When there were no pills or other contraceptive methods so that women were pregnant a lot of the time, when there was no bread in stores so that women had to spend hours doing their own baking, when women had no legal rights, when nobody would give a woman a job, when women aged early and died young from too much work and too much childbearing, when, in many parts of the world, men bought and sold women as slaves, prostitutes, or concubines — there often was no choice but to submit to one's fate and be grateful it was no worse.

But now that women have more rights, now that doors have been opened (the doors get stuck from time to time when a male foot gets planted firmly on the other side — but they can be opened if a few women get together and give a good, hard shove), now that it is possible to expand our lives, there is no longer any necessity to settle for a new microwave oven as the high point of one's existence. Now that we have the legal rights women fought for, it is time to honor, not betray, as Carolyn Heilbrun says, our grandmothers, mothers, daughters, sisters who have been treated as disposable and defrauded for generations of brave but hidden lives. We must reward their efforts and bravery with our work and our freedom. We must change women's lives to change the world. If you start, she says, by changing your own life, sooner or later it will help another girl change hers.

Yet many women, untrained for independence and programmed only for wifehood and motherhood, go on accepting an inferior, dependent role, go on accepting the depression that comes first when they are trapped in their homes and afterward when their children grow up and they find nothing to do in their empty nests. They never discover how joyous and exciting a relationship between a man and woman can be when they share not only their bodies but their minds, when the two face each other as equals instead of playing the game (often not even true) or big-man-little-woman.

There is an old saying that a man divides his time between his work and his marriage, while for a woman, marriage is her whole life. A pretty unfair arrangement, but it can be stopped. No man is going to give up his work or his outside interests to even the score. So it remains for a woman to find interesting work or have outside interests also.

Some women say, "I haven't got time to do anything else. The house and its occupants keeps me busy from morning till night."

Betty Friedan, who wrote a book called *The Feminine Mystique*, discovered something interesting when she interviewed housewives around the country. She discovered that housework expands to fill whatever time you want to give to it. Women who worked and who only gave a few hours a week to their housework kept their houses just as clean, enjoyed meals just as well cooked, and set up a household routine just as smooth as housewives who stayed home. They didn't change their sheets five times a week or scrub a floor that didn't need scrubbing or bake bread they didn't need just to fill the hours of the day.

Some housewives say, "I don't feel I have any right to complain. Housework may be boring, but my husband's job is just as boring." Maybe, but he's being paid for it!

No matter which way you look at it, for most women in developed countries where there is plenty of machinery (we do not speak of women struggling in ricefields so their children can eat at all), housewifing is simply not enough and not rewarding enough to fill a lifetime. And more and more women are coming to accept this. Alone in the kitchen is a place more and more women don't want to stay.

Look at those questions we asked at the end of the intro-duction: why didn't the women's Second Wave liberation movement of 1965-1975 entirely work? And why, with laws pretty much in place about sex discrimination and harass-ment and equal opportunity in education, jobs, and pay, why has so much not changed for girls and women, why do we continue in second place and need the current Third Wave liberation movement to work better?

Now do you understand more deeply the answer? Gender is not destiny. You can teach boys what girls know. You can teach girls what boys know. We may be born a little gender-different, psychologically as well as physically, but girls and boys are equally smart and can learn one another's qualities.

Why hasn't it changed? As we said, *attitude*. It seems that while the human brain can work miracles like spaceships and cathedrals, it has a hard time changing its attitude.

Section Two

HOW WE GOT THIS WAY

Adam And Eve

Young men and women in schools, colleges, and universities all over the world are fighting today against being limited to traditional sex roles.

Girls have begun to reject being trained to be servants, and boys have begun to reject being trained to be money machines.

There are students, male and female alike, who now value individual fulfillment of whatever talents, capacities, goals they have. Both sexes encourage each other to do what interests them. Accomplishment is beginning to be no longer limited to the male. And both sexes, not just females, are learning to value the warmth of human relationships. If independence and serious commitment are good values, they are good values for women as well as men. If sensitivity and emotional warmth are good values, they are good values not only for women but for men as well.

In many young marriages, both the man and the woman have jobs or professions, and both share equally the cooking and household chores. The Me-Tarzan-I-Bring-Home-The-Nuts-And-Berries-You-Jane-You-Cook-The-Nuts-And-Berries recipe for marriage, the breadwinner-homemaker image of the married couple, is fading .

But it isn't fading without a struggle. We have been propagandized for too many thousands of years. And some parents are still rearing their children to fit the popular stereotypes. Think, for a moment, about what ideas you've been brought up on, and how early in life you were fed those ideas, and how you were never told this was only one of many sets of ideas in the world but that THIS WAS THE ONLY RIGHT WAY TO LIVE!

Think, for a moment, of the Bible.

"In the beginning God created the heavens and the earth. Then God said, Let us make man in our image, after our likeness; and let them have dominion...over all the earth...and the rib which the Lord God had taken from the man he made into a woman and brought her to the man....Then the Lord God said to the woman, What is this that you have done? The woman said, The serpent beguiled me, and I ate....To the woman He said, I will greatly multiply your pain in child-bearing; in pain you shall bring forth

children, yet your desire shall be for your husband, and he
shall rule over you." (Genesis 1,2,3.)

St. Paul seconds the motion about who is to rule over
whom, and whose is the greater glory.

"For a man ought not to cover his head, since he is the im-
age and glory of God; but woman is the glory of man. For
man was not made from woman, but woman from man.
Neither was man created for woman, but woman for man."
(Corinthians 1:11.)

If the Christians taught male superiority, the Jews were
no better. So lowly did they think the status of women that
one Orthodox Jewish prayer goes like this:

Blessed art Thou, oh Lord our God, King of the Universe,
that I was not born a gentile.
Blessed art Thou, oh Lord our God, King of the Universe,
that I was not born a slave.
Blessed art Thou, oh Lord our God, King of the Universe,
that I was not born a woman.

And in the Moslem Koran:

"Men are superior to women on account of the qualities in
which God has given them preeminence."

Clearly, it has never occurred to men that another inter-
pretation of the story of Adam and Eve is possible. When

God began creating things, he created them in the order of their importance, saving his greatest creation until last. When men tell the story of creation, they talk of Adam as being the highest of God's creations, and Eve as an afterthought. But since, in actual sequence, Eve was the last to be created, why not think of *her* as the crowning achievement of God's creativity?

And as for the business with the apple, men have always ignored its significance. Disobedient or not, it was Eve who took the first bite, and thereby she became the person who brought knowledge and curiosity into the world.

The myth of male superiority has been taught in many ways and enforced for thousands of years. Ever since our ancestors lived in caves and men decided they were superior because they had bigger muscles, they have cowed women into submission and believed that men were a higher order of being.

The Greeks had a myth, "Pandora's Box," in which it was said that a woman was responsible for all the suffering in the world. Two of the greatest Greek thinkers, Plato and Aristotle, had horrid things to say about women. Plato was so convinced of all women's lack of intelligence that he wasn't sure they shouldn't be classed as animals. Aristotle went so far as to suggest women might have been born by mistake. Another Greek, Menander, said, "A woman is necessarily an evil, but he that gets the most tolerable one is lucky."

Orthodox Jews considered women unclean.

Early Christians were taught by St. Paul, "It is not good for a man to touch a woman." They were told by St. Augustine that a woman was like a temple built over a sewer.

Moslems were told by Mohammed that "when Eve was created, Satan rejoiced."

Hindus were told, "A woman must never be free of subjugation."

There's even a Buddhist sect that considers women the result of imperfect karma.

Since people today are still being taught to read (without questioning the images presented) the writings of the Greek philosophers, and the religious writings of the past, is it any wonder that the status of women has greatly suffered because of it?

By the Middle Ages, Western churchmen were arguing over whether women even had souls. The church, as well as society, had become completely male dominated, and the Protestant Reformation, when it came along in the sixteenth century, did nothing to help.

Martin Luther believed not only that women were secondary to men, but that sexuality was Original Sin. John Calvin said woman's only useful function was to bear children, and he spoke out against political equality for women.

The great poet John Milton called women a "defect of nature."

For centuries, there were brutal attacks on women who were thought to be in league with the devil. These were often women who were healers, who were independent enough to live unprotected by church or marriage, who were of exceptional intelligence and were called witches. Such women were burned at the stake. Even the great military leader Joan of Arc was burned for being a heretic. She would never have been burned if she had been a man.

In the eighteenth century, during the period of Enlightenment, men were still writing horrid things about women. They may have formulated ideas of freedom for themselves, but they did nothing to release women from bondage.

The French philosopher Rousseau wrote that it was necessary to discipline women so that they would be obedient to men. He said it was "necessary to accustom them early to such confinement, that it may not afterward cost them too dear; and to the suppression of their caprices that they may the more readily submit to the will of others." He also wrote, "She ought to learn even to suffer injustices and to bear the insults of a husband without complaint."

Diderot, another French philosopher, wrote, "Women prefer lustful, depraved men because women are depraved and lustful."

Lord Chesterfield, a famous womanhater, wrote advice to his son.

> *"Women, then, are only children of a larger growth; they have an entertaining tattle, and sometimes wit; but for solid reasoning, good sense, I never knew in my life one that had it.... A man of sense only trifles with them, plays with them, humors and flatters them...but he neither consults them about, nor trusts them with serious matters...Women have*

in truth but two passions, vanity and love; these are their universal characters."

Even the great American liberal Thomas Jefferson said in 1807, "The appointment of a woman to office is an innovation for which the public is not prepared — nor am I."

The poet Tennyson wrote, "Woman is the lesser man."

George Meredith: "I expect that Woman will be the last thing civilized by Man."

Schopenhauer called women "childish, frivolous, and short-sighted."

Nietzsche said, "When you go to a woman, do not forget to take along your whip." It was in Hitler's Germany that modern woman-hating was the worst. Hitler even declared that woman's emancipation was a Jewish plot. The Nazi movement was declared to be a masculine movement, and women were denied voting rights and the right to hold public office. They were told their only acceptable activities were children, kitchen, and church.

In the early part of this century, Alfred Adler, a Viennese psychiatrist wrote, "All our institutions, our traditional attitudes, our laws, our morals, our customs, give evidence of the fact that they are determined and maintained by the privileged males for the glory of male domination....They believe that women are here only for the purpose of being submissive."

Although it is quite true that laws and customs and values are changing, that people are beginning to understand that just because men have muscles it doesn't given them the right to rule over women (and those muscles are about as useful in our modern push-button society as an appendix), and although our twentieth century democratic philosophies have developed new ideas about the equality of every human being, it's still going to take a while to change things if people keep thinking the same old nonsense.

The Bound Foot

For a couple of million years, human beings lived by hunting and gathering their food. They hunted and caught wild animals when they could. They gathered and ate wild fruit, nuts, leaves, roots, eggs, and insects.

Tarzanists believe that in those early times the women and children spent their days lolling about the cave waiting for the big man to come home from his dangerous and exhausting hunt with a lion between his teeth. George Bernard Shaw put these words into the mouth of Cain in his play *Back to Methuselah*:

"I will hunt: I will fight and strive to the very bursting of my sinews. When I have slain the boar at the risk of my life, I will throw it to the woman to cook, and give her a morsel of it for her pains. She shall have no other food, and that will make her my slave....Man shall be the master of Woman."

This is, of course, just silly. It was never like that, and among surviving hunting communities it is not like that now. Studies of the tribal peoples in the Kalahari Desert of Africa show that hunting is often slow and unpredictable, and that vegetable foods gathered by the women comprise from 60 to 80 percent of the total diet of everyone. Outside the Arctic, this 60 to 80 percent holds true for all hunting-gathering groups studied to date.

Women in primitive societies were of primary economic importance. It is generally accepted now that, owing to her ancient role as the gatherer of vegetable foods, woman was responsible for the invention and development of agriculture. Many paleoanthropologists think it was very probably the female homonid with a baby on her hip who ventured out of the shrinking African rainforest onto the savannah 3 or 4 million years ago (our own genus Homo replaced these early Australopithecus hominids perhaps 2 million years ago). That female, looking for food for herself and her baby could not have stayed alive had she not stood up tall enough to see lions and other predators coming through the savannah grass. The rotating hip, the use of her memory to image the lion so she could run for safety sooner the next time — all of this enlarged the human brain — and only those whose brains enlarged survived to reproduce the rest of us, also with enlarged brains.

What I am getting at here is not just another lesson in the science of anthropology. What I am getting at is that there is every evidence that the female of our species was the first to enlarge the human brain as well as the first agronomist and environmentalist and the first farmer.

The invention of agriculture about 10,000 years ago was an important revolution, because with food readily available there was time to improve tools, invent handwriting, and develop all the arts and sciences that made for civilization. The women of the New Stone Age, because they brought forth food from the earth and children from their bodies, were worshipped and given status, as the widespread remains of shrines and the clay statues of the Mother Goddess from Southwest Asia to Europe prove. Anthropologists have discovered that in many non-Western cultures — among the Hopi Indians; in Burma, Indonesia, and in certain African tribes below the Sahara — women have had more freedom and equality than in the more technologically advanced civilizations of Asia, Europe, and the United States.

It was our invention of agriculture that produced the leisure necessary for the basis of civilization. We didn't have to go running around quite so much to find food. It takes time to think up math and science, the language and writing to communicate the information gathered, the laws and institutions necessary for sedentary groups of people to live together or fight for their territory.

It was our invention of agriculture that did us women in, too. More of our babies lived. We lived longer to produce more babies. Now there wasn't just one baby. There was a baby at the breast, one at the hip, one at the ankles, and one on the way. We made the deal with the men that threw our independence and power away forever, that threw us into our isolated kitchens and separated us from one another. "You cope with the fields." we said, "and bring home the food. I've got my hands full of babies to feed and diapers to wash and the cooking and...." Well, you know the rest. The men took the extra food to market, earning the money, bonding with the other guys, forming football teams and governments, making up all the rules. One of the male rules was marriage. Oh, yes, they invented marriage. If you want to leave your land and property to children you know are really yours, you better own the baby factory and keep the key. As for us? It's ten thousand years later. I think we have to cut a new deal. Call the new deal, Let's Take Turns.

Although women played so great a part in producing bigger brains, more food, and civilization, their status changed with the coming of male rulers and priests (the men wanted male gods), with city living (the men wanted male kings and clubs), and military conquests (the men had all the weapons). Records show that even in the great early civilizations of Egypt, Babylonia, Greece, Rome, India, China, and Japan, men dominated women, treated them as property, and used them mainly for childbearing or for pleasure. With agriculture, and the domestication of food and animals, we lost our wildness and our personal independence. Agriculture, and,

with it, the beginning of technology, the extensive possessions of land, houses, cattle, equipment, was not necessarily
a good deal for women, or for the human race. The subse-
quent money economy (and as we no longer produced food,
we had no money) left us totally dependent. From that time
on the position of women varied little, until the late nineteenth century.

Not only have women in major civilizations had no political rights; not only have they been ranted at by orators
and writers who called them inferiors, animals, mindless,
and the source of sin; not only have they attained rights and
then had them taken away again; not only all this, but they
have suffered physical bondage and punishment as well.

For a thousand years, up to early days of this century,
Chinese girls, as we have mentioned, had their feet
bound in childhood, at six or seven years of age. Lengths of
bandage were wrapped around the four smaller toes and
the heel, very tightly, in order to bend the toes under the
foot and make the arch high and bowed. An ideal foot was
three inches long. To attain this, little girls suffered intense
pain. Pus and blood often dripped from their bandages, their
toes broke. And once their feet were bound they were never
able to run about. In fact, girls and women could barely
hobble around; they had to use walls, canes, and the support of others even to move about the house. A Chinese
woman's life was spent modestly concealed indoors, and if
she went out, she went in a curtained sedan chair. Although
this crippling device was supposed to make the woman

beautiful, a Chinese manual gives a more practical purpose. "Why are feet bound? It is not because they are good looking with their bowed arch, but rather because men feared that women might easily leave their quarters and therefore had their feet bound tightly in order to prevent this." In China, women were often a man's property, bought as concubines or slaves. A man did not want the chastity of his property damaged, so he made certain his women could not move very far.

In Moslem countries, for centuries women were confined to harems, or women's apartments. The women were veiled and kept in strict seclusion from the world. A man might have four wives and as many concubines as he could afford; his power over them was absolute. In some Arab countries, women are still bought and sold into harems, and a man's power over the lives of women in his harem is still absolute.

In some African tribes (we have told the story of the beautiful supermodel who escaped her nomadic Somalian tribe), women were and still are mutilated (their clitorises cut off) to prevent them from feeling sexual pleasure and their vaginas sewn up to guard their chastity (the 2 million girls a year who are subjected to this ritual are offered up by their own mothers!)

Forceful restraint and punishment of women was not confined to the East and Near East. When medieval knights went off to war or on Crusades, they had a habit of locking metal chastity belts around the waists and between the legs of their wives in order to ensure that they behaved properly while their masters were away. Physical punishment then was also perfectly legal, and a man had every right to beat his women. Church law permitted husbands to beat their women with whips and sticks (not, however, with iron weapons).

The ancient Hebrews sold their daughters into marriage. Babylonians auctioned off women to the high bidders. In ancient Greece, Athenian women were confined to their homes. Not only could they not vote (all that Greek democracy was only for Athenian men) they could not even appear in the streets. (In Sparta, women were a little better off. They could own land. On occasion, they even had two husbands.) In ancient Rome, women had rights over their own property, but men had the power of life and death over the women.

Christians borrowed the Hebrew attitude toward women and gradually took away what few rights the Roman women had gained. The jurists of the Middle Ages made a pronouncement that women could have no personal identity, and in England it was "adjudged that the wife has nothing of her own while her husband lives."

Men throughout the ages who possessed unusual wisdom were called prophets, seers, philosophers. Women who possessed unusual wisdom or who dared to be different were generally called witches, and in the seventeenth century especially, many such women in Europe and America were hanged or burned at the stake.

For thousands of years, particularly in the Near East and Far East, though it happened in Europe too, families could sell their daughters as prostitutes into brothels or as slaves. Selling females, legally or not, is still practiced in some parts of the world. Selling girls and women into brothels was even done in Victorian England, less than a hundred years ago, and in the America's. In the early part of this century, especially, white slavery flourished. During WWII, German Nazis forced Jewish women to sexually service their troops; Japan forced their own and Chinese and Korean women into "comfort" stations to sexually serve their own soldiers. And the viciousness with which black women were treated in all areas where black slavery flourished is among the greatest horrors of Western history.

It's true that through history, there have been great women. There have been great rulers like Cleopatra of Egypt, Elizabeth and Victoria of England, Catherine of Russia, various empresses of China and Japan, in our own day Golda Meir of Israel, Indira Gandhi of India, Bhutto of Pakistan, Bandaranaike of Sri Lanka. Thousands of women have been important powers behind the political scene. There have been important women writers, important women scientists, important women in religion. The trouble is, that for all their importance, they made no permanent difference in women's rights. Give or take a few primitive societies, women have remained dominated and subjugated by men. In no major society are women treated as equals to this day.

As the United Nations reported in 1995, "In the household, women are the last to eat. At school, they are the last to be educated. At work, they are the last to be hired and the first to be fired. And from childhood through adulthood, they are abused because of their gender....One-third of wives in developing countries are physically battered. One woman in 2,000 in the world is reported to have been raped: 40,000 in former Yugoslavia alone, where just recently rape was an accepted act of war. In the U.S., there were more than 150,000 reported rapes in 1993. In India…9,000 dowry-related deaths each year." If these numbers reflect their reported instances, just think how many more go unreported and unrecorded. Another United Nations study of domestic violence showed that in many developing countries, women would often stay in a violent relationship, because at least they knew who would rape and beat them. Without a man, such women would be vulnerable to violence from all men.

This is no way to live.

The Empty Mind

Throughout history, we have lacked most of the legal rights of men. We have lacked political representation. We have been confined, sold, and mutilated. Even when we have been treated well, white women particularly have been thought of as children, not adults.

A question that is often raised is, "Well, if women were so discontented with their lot, whey didn't they strike out on their own?"

The answer to that is, "With what!"

The most important tool for getting anywhere in this world, aside from personal freedom, is training, mentoring— education.

While it is true that in most civilizations, many women of the upper classes were taught to red and write, in the past women in general had little or no education at all. Even among the upper classes, women's education was confined primarily to such feminine arts as embroidery, a little singing, the playing of a musical instrument, or dabbling in art. Women were seldom taught anything they could use to make a living. They were even advised that it was unfeminine to do any one thing very well. In less developed communities, Nepal as an example, women and their daughters are often too exhausted from producing up to 90% of the food to have time for anything else. It is service, not intellect, that has been valued in women.

A Mrs. Ellis gave exactly that warning to young women in her book *The Family Monitor and Domestic Guide*, which was widely read in England and the United States in the middle of the nineteenth century.

> *It must not be supposed that the writer is one who would advocate as essential to woman, any very extraordinary degree of intellectual attainment, especially if confined to one particular branch of study....To be able to do a great many things tolerably well, is of infinitly more value to a woman, than to be able to excel in any one.*

It was simply not ladylike to draw attention to oneself by doing anything very well.

St. Paul said women should listen in silence and be taught by their husbands— but he meant their duty, not science and mathematics.

In the nineteenth century, Rousseau belittled women's intellectual abilities. "Almost all of them learn with reluctance to read and write; but very readily apply themselves to the use of their needles." He felt that it was useless to teach women to think because their minds were unfit for abstract thought, and that women's entire education ought to be confined to learning to please men.

(In actual fact, UN studies of developing countries have proved that investing in girls' early education improves the productivity of agriculture in particular and the general GNP much more than the same investment for boys. We learn faster, stay in school longer, and because we have been taught duty, patience, and application as females, we use those qualities to apply education to productivity.)

But up to a hundred years ago, sexism had it that women's brains were smaller in relation to their size than men's brains and therefore less able. Alexander Walker wrote about beauty in women in 1837 and concluded that the ideal beauty's head ought to be small "because the mental system in the female ought to be subordinate to the vital."

There is a German proverb that says: "A woman has the form of an angel...and the mind of an ass."

It was thought that an intellectual woman was unfeminine. Nietsche said, "When a woman inclines to learning there is usually something wrong with her sex apparatus."

Lady Mary Wortley Montagu advised her daughter to hide her learning "like a physical defect."

Note that most women went along with all this nonsense!

So because men thought we had inferior minds to begin with, and because they felt threatened by intelligent women, women were simply left uneducated for anything but household work and motherhood and a little graceful dabbling on the side.

Among many African nomadic tribes, women not only produce 90% of the food but build the houses and make the clothes. You might wonder why they respect or even need their men at all, much less obey. But they do. And Latourette says of the education of Chinese women (or rather lack of it) up until this century that while many in wealthy families were given some tutoring, most women were illiterate. Girls were primarily educated in the management of a household, in ceremonial duties, in courtesy, and in the proprieties and rituals. Women's sphere was believed to be in the home.

To underscore the fact that it was our oppression, not our faculties, that were at fault, in two countries where women were most confined, in China and in the Arab countries, women often ran brisk businesses from their homes and hid the proceeds from their husbands. Recently, Arab feminists, now literate, earning money — in Saudi Arabia, controlling nearly half of the assets — began to claim their rights by unveiling and going out into the world, quoting the story of Khadija, the first wife of the Prophet Mohammed, whose business earnings had supported her husband while he went out to preach.

In Europe, too, women were barred from all but the most elementary of education. The girls of better families were taught to read and write, but were refused entrance into all institutions of higher learning. An exceptional woman might have herself tutored or teach herself more than was usual, but this was rare.

Occasionally a lonely woman raised a voice in protest. Lady Winchilsea, a seventeenth-century Englishwoman wrote:

How are we fallen! Fallen by mistaken rules
And Education's more than Nature's fools;
Debarred from all improvements of the mind
And to be dull, expected and designed
And if some one would soar above the rest,
With warmer fancy and ambitions pressed,
So strong the opposing faction still appears,
The hopes to thrive can ne'er outweigh the fears.

Not only did women remain uneducated, but those few who did manage to use their intellects were shamed, made to feel unwomanly and afraid of criticism.

It was toward the end of the eighteenth century that the protest to free women and to give them an education began to grow. It is hardly a coincidence that the struggle to free women began in America just after the Revolutionary War and grew strong at the time of the Civil War when women helped fight to free the African Americans from slavery.

Thomas Paine, spokesman for the Revolution, was among the first to condemn, in 1775, the position of women. He said, "even in countries where they may be esteemed the most happy, [women are]…robbed of freedom and will by the laws, the slaves of opinion."

Mary Wollstonecraft (mother of Mary Shelley who wrote *Frankenstein*) spearheaded the feminist movement in England. She said in 1792 in her book *Vindication of the Rights of Women* that it was hardly surprising that women concentrated on the way they looked instead of what was in their minds since not much had been put into their minds to begin with.

In America ten years earlier, Judith Sargent Murray said women needed knowledge to envision new goals and grow by reaching for them.

Finally, there was a coeducational college — Oberlin, founded in 1832. But even at Oberlin, the administrators decided women's minds couldn't cope with the same courses as men, and they were given a special literary course. The great feminist Lucy Stone, who attended Oberlin, wrote:

Oberlin's attitude was that women's high calling was to be the mothers of the race….If women became lawyers, ministers, physicians, lecturers, politicians or any sort of "public character," the home would suffer from neglect….

Washing the men's clothes, caring for their rooms, serving them at table, listening to their orations, but themselves re-

maining respectfully silent in public assemblages, the Oberlin "co-eds" were being prepared for intelligent motherhood and a properly subservient wifehood.

Lucy Stone had been inspired to seek an education for herself when she heard Mary Lyon speak of education for women at a church sewing circle. Mary Lyon had been traveling all through New England collecting money in order to found a woman's college. She started Mount Holyoke, which, in 1837, opened its doors to give women their first chance at education equal to a man's. The women learned mathematics, the sciences, history, philosophy — not how to be better wives and mothers. Because women were not admitted to the great men's universities, toward the end of the century more women's colleges were founded — Vassar, Smith, Wellesley, Bryn Mawr.

Women — and even a few men who realized that half the human race was being denied the right to become fully human — had finally begun to fight the conditions that had enslaved them for centuries, the conditions summed up by the first Woman's Rights Convention in Seneca Falls, New York, in 1848. The women said of man:

He has compelled her to submit to laws in the formation of which she has no voice....He has made her, if married, in the eyes of the law, civilly dead. He has taken from her all right to property, even to the wages she earns....He closes against her all the avenues of wealth and distinction which he con-

siders most honorable to himself....He has denied her the facilities for obtaining a thorough education, all colleges being closed against her.

But when we got our own colleges at last, there were still more steps to be taken. Without the right to vote, women still had no real power. As M. Carey Thomas, the brilliant first president of Bryn Mawr, said in 1908:

Women are one-half the world, but until a century ago...women lived a twilight life, a half life apart, and looked out and saw men as shadows walking. It was a man's world. The laws were men's laws, the government a man's government, the country a man's country. Now women have won the right to higher education and economic independence. The right to become citizens of the state is the next and inevitable consequence of education and work outside the home. We have gone so far; we must go farther. We cannot go back.

The right to education was the first necessity. The feminists of the last century who fought for women's rights to higher education, careers, the vote, understood that it was necessary to shatter the image of woman as a silly, useless decoration to own, as a passive, mindless animal to drudge, as a brood cow, as someone incapable of making her own decisions about her life. It had to be proved that women were fully human. It had to be proved that women needed a sense of their own identity, as men had always had. It had to be proved that women were the equals of men. And for that education was essential.

Yet there are still people who question the "fitness" of fully educating women. There are still men — and women! — who think of girls as feeble-minded creatures in need of protection whose only destiny is to breed babies. These are the people who want to prevent women from taking full part in the shaping of the world, who still insist that women remain "outsiders." Men who hang on to this notion want to preserve their privileges of entitlement and exploitation of women, the world, the natural environment, all they can. Women who hang on to this notion want to exploit men into handing over what has been exploited.

There was a play, written by Henrik Ibsen, in 1879, called *A Doll's House*. Women in Europe and America for nearly a hundred years have identified themselves with Nora, when they hear her say:

> *You have always been so kind to me. But our home has been nothing but a playroom. I have been your doll wife, just as at home I was Papa's doll child; and here the children have been my dolls....How am I fitted to bring up the children?... There is another task I must undertake first. I must try and educate myself — you are not the man to help me in that. I must do that for myself.*

Her husband is horrified that Nora is leaving him and reminds her that before all else she is a wife and mother. Nora answers:

I believe that before all else I am a reasonable human being, just as you are — or, at all events, that I must try and become one.

Indeed, before all else we must make of ourselves reasonable human beings.

And then make reason heard. As a young, black, pregnant Philadelphian teenage girl recently wrote to Hillary Carlip for the collection of teenage girls' writings in her book *Girl Power*:

It was hard enough to get in a good school, much less get a good job. I do feel very oppressed because there are too many male chauvinists running the show. They feel that women never were, aren't now, and never will be their equal on the work force....I am upset because I plan on bringing a child into a chaotic world that I have minimal say in....I really hope I can make a difference...through my writing.

The fight goes on!

The Feminist Struggle

In a discussion with a group of teenage girls on the subject of women's liberation we said, "The aim of American feminism is the overthrow of the oldest and most rigid class system in existence, the class system based on sex."

One of the girls nodded in happy approval and then said, "What I still don't understand is why it took women so long to decide to fight back."

Part of the answer is that until the Industrial Revolution in the nineteenth century, it was impossible for most women, no matter how free they wished to be, to find work that would allow them to be financially independent of men. Until the nineteenth century, all circumstances combined to keep even the few educated women at home. Society urgently needed women to bear and care for children and did everything it could to make sure women stayed home and did just that.

Another of the girls asked why we didn't shoot our way out of the house. The answer to that is women are conditioned to be peace-keepers (which is why our children don't kill each other in the nursery) not warriors. And we did not bond together. Women's conditioning is to bond to men, not to each other.

It took the Industrial Revolution with its growth of factories — and because of the factories, the need for a larger work force — to create enough jobs for women. And then it took, in this century, the discovery of effective methods of birth control, to free us from constant pregnancy. It is necessary, in order to fight for freedom without violence, to be able to earn your own living, to communicate with others in like position, and to be able to control your own body. (These are the reasons why, although women need liberating everywhere, feminism began in technologically developed countries.)

It was in the middle of the nineteenth century, with industrialization in full swing, that the first full-fledged feminist movement got underway. It's not surprising that the active struggle for women's freedom began in America. We were a young country, less bound by tradition than other lands. We had just come through the American Revolution, with its ideals of freedom. We were confronted with the Civil War and the abolitionist struggle to free slaves. Freedom was in the air, and American women began to decide they wanted it for themselves.

It was in the cause of antislavery that women first got together politically. In 1837, the year Mount Holyoke opened, American women held their first national antislavery convention in New York. Then in 1840, Elizabeth Cady Stanton (on her honeymoon) and Lucretia Mott (mother of five), met in London at an antislavery convention. When they arrived, Mott, Stanton, and the rest of the delegation of American women were barred from taking part in the convention and were shut off behind a curtain in the back gallery. At that point, the women decided it wasn't only their African-American brothers and sisters who needed to be freed.

Eight years later, in 1848, Mott and Stanton organized the first convention on women's rights in Seneca Falls. The Seneca Falls Declaration was modeled on the Declaration of Independence and lists the grievances and sufferings of women everywhere.

> *The history of mankind is a history of repeated injuries and usurpations on the part of man toward woman, having in direct object the establishment of an absolute tyranny over her...*
>
> *He has never permitted her to exercise her inalienable right to the elective franchise.*
>
> *He has compelled her to submit to laws in the formation of which she had no voice.*

He has withheld from her rights which are given to the most ignorant and degraded men — both natives and foreigners.

Having deprived her of this first right of a citizen...he has oppressed her on all sides.

He has made her, if married, in the eye of the law, civilly dead.

He has taken from her all right in property, even to the wages she earns.

...she is compelled to promise obedience to her husband, he becoming to all intents and purposes, her master — the law giving him power to deprive her of her liberty and to administer chastisement.

After depriving her of all rights as a married woman, if single and the owner of property, he has taxed her....

He has monopolized nearly all the profitable employments....He closes against her all the avenues to wealth and distinction....

He has denied her the facilities for obtaining a thorough education, all colleges being closed against her.

There were more grievances on women's lack of place in religion, their persecution morally under the double standard, their deprivation under circumstances of divorce, the inferior and abject life they were forced to lead. They insisted "that they have immediate admission to all the rights and privileges which belong to them as citizens of the United States."

The newspapers ridiculed the women of Seneca Falls and called them aged spinsters who could not find husbands. But despite the ridicule and the name calling, in the years that followed, women's rights conventions and meetings were held throughout the country. And here and there, they received male support. In Boston, in 1853, the Reverend Theodore Parker preached: "To make one-half the human race consume its energies in the functions of housekeeper, wife and mother is a monstrous waste of the most precious material God ever made."

As if to echo Reverend Parker's words, there is a banner on the wall of a San Francisco classroom whose teacher is trying not only to practice equity but to teach it, to change both boy's and girls' perspectives on the female self, and this to 60% white, 40% Latino, Filipino, Asian-American, African-American sixth graders. The banner is surround by images of women — Harriet Tubman and Sojourner Truth, Anita Hill and Sally Ride, Gloria Steinem and Rosa Parks, Susan Anthony and Lucretia Mott, and books on artist Judy Chicago's famous "Dinner Party" as well as scientist Rosalind Franklin's experiments (Franklin discovered the double helix, the structure of DNA but she had died of cancer, and two men named Watson and Crick walked off with what should have been Franklin's Nobel Prize), stories of the three women, Jane Goodall, Dian Fossey, and Birute Galdikas whose decades-long studies of the great primates changed the way we study wildlife and understand our relationship to other primates forever — all this is under a giant banner that reads:

WOMEN ARE ONE-HALF OF THE WORLD'S PEOPLE; THEY DO TWO-THIRDS OF THE WORLD'S WORK; THEY EARN ONE-TENTH OF THE WORLD'S INCOME; THEY OWN ONE ONE-HUNDREDTH OF THE WORLD'S PROPERTY. (from Peggy Orenstein's *SchoolGirls*)

Despite the opposition they faced, many women went on struggling for the right even to vote. They lobbied, lectured, held parades, demonstrated, and gathered petitions in their effort to introduce suffrage for women into Congress. Antifeminists called them unnatural, man-eating monsters and reported them as big, mannish women who smoked cigars and swore like troopers. It was true many of the early feminists cut their hair short and wore bloomers and tried to be like men. Why not? They saw the pitiable lives their mothers led and had every reason to reject the traditional image of women.

Lucy Stone, who, with Elizabeth Cady Stanton and Susan B. Anthony, was among the foremost leaders of the early women's rights movement, was a small feminine woman with a gentle voice. She lectured on abolition Saturdays and Sundays, as an agent for the Anti-Slavery Society,. and during the rest of the week, on women's rights. Although she was described as "a prototype of womanly grace," men threatened her with clubs, threw eggs at her, and once in the middle of winter, pushed a hose through a window and sprayed her with icy water. Although Lucy Stone had said, "Marriage is to a woman a state of slavery," she did finally marry. But she and her husband agreed to a special pact at the ceremony — there was to be no vow of obedience and no superiority on the part of the husband. Afterward, Lucy Stone kept her own name, in fear that to become a wife was to die as a person.

Susan B. Antony, brilliant leader of the suffrage movement, never married, but devoted her life to the cause. She declared,

> *By law, public sentiment and religion from the time of Moses down to the present day, woman has never been thought of other than as a piece of property, to be disposed of at the will and pleasure of man. Women must be educated out of their unthinking acceptance of financial dependence on man into mental and economic independence. [Women must not] sell themselves — in marriage or out — for bread and shelter.*

When men scoffed at the suffragists and said women had it easy because men were so chivalrous toward them, Elizabeth Cady Stanton (who wrote a *Woman's Bible* to disprove what she considered misinterpretations about women in the Bible) was outraged. She said,

> *Talk not to us of chivalry, that died long ago...a man in love will jump to pick up a glove or bouquet for a silly girl of sixteen, whilst at home he will permit his aged mother to carry pails of water and armfuls of wood or his wife to lug a twenty-pound baby, hour after hour, without ever offering to relieve her.*

Angelina Grimke, another great fighter for women's rights answered the question of chivalry this way. "I ask no favors for my sex. I surrender not our claim to equality. All I ask of our brethren is that they will take their feet from off our necks and permit us to stand upright on the ground which God has designed us to occupy!"

Alice Stone Blackwell, Lucy Stone's daughter, remarked, "Justice is better than chivalry if we cannot have both."

But it was Sojourner Truth — who had been born into slavery, was freed, and along with Harriet Tubman, went back time and again with a huge price on her head to free other slaves — who made perhaps the most moving statement of all when men talked about how chivalrous they were toward the "frailty" of women.

The man over there says women need to be helped into carriages and lifted over ditches, and to have the best places everywhere. Nobody ever helps me into carriages, or over puddles, or gives me the best place — and ain't I a woman? Look at my arm! I have ploughed and planted and gathered into barns and no man could head me — and ain't I a woman? I could work as much and eat as much as a man — when I could get it — and bear the lash as well! And ain't I a woman? I have borne thirteen children, and seen most of 'em sold into slavery, and when I cried out with my mother's grief, none but Jesus heard me — and ain't I a woman?

The sad part of the early feminist struggle was that while the battle to free the slaves was being won, the battle for women's rights got nowhere. Sojourner Truth said, "There is a great stir about colored men getting their rights, but not a word about colored women; and if colored men get their rights, and not colored women theirs, you see the colored men will be masters over the women, and it will be just as bad as it was before."

It was true for white women as well.

When the war was over, the black men got the vote. But not the black women. Nor the white women, either.

During their lifetimes, the pioneer feminists saw the laws of almost every state change toward women: high schools opened to them, and two-thirds of the colleges in the United States, white women, that is. But it took another generation to finish the battle for woman's vote, and another hundred years for the Civil Rights movement to open educations doors for African-American women.

As the fight to free women was spurred on by the fight to free slaves in the nineteenth century, so in the twentieth century it was spurred on by the fight for others kinds of social reform. The new feminists fought against the horrible working conditions in factories, against child labor, and for the rise of unions.

The final battle for the vote was led by Carrie Chapman Catt, a teacher and a newspaperwoman. In 1913, tens of thousands of suffragists marched in torchlight parades in New York, Boston, Chicago, and Washington, D.C. In Washington, nearly ten thousand women marched on the White House. The police did nothing while mobs attacked the women, knocking them down, slapping them, throwing burning cigar stubs at them. They were beaten and blood-ied and dragged off to hospitals and jails. A group of women who chained themselves to the White House fence were ar-rested and dragged away to jail. They went on hunger strikes and were martyred by forced feeding.

While this was happening in America, a similar struggle was going on in other countries. The battle in England was even bloodier than here. Women broke windows, poured acid into mailboxes, and attacked members of Parliament with stones and whips. In return the women were brutally treated in jail.

But despite the hostility they met, the feminists went on fighting and winning adherents. The organizations formed to work for the vote had about two millions members throughout the country. And at last the effort paid off.

The Nineteenth Amendment to the United States Consti-tution was signed on August 26, 1920, and gave 26 million women the right to vote. But even then it took two more years to get the amendment ratified! And it was 1922 before the Supreme Court finally ruled that women could vote.

Carrie Chapman Catt had worked not only for American women. In 1904, she had helped to organize the International Woman Suffrage Alliance, and by 1920, when we won our vote so had the women of twenty-two other countries.

But with victory, came tragedy. With the winning of the vote, the feminist movement died. Some of the women went on to form the League of Women Voters, but the League can only lobby, not elect. Women had the vote, but they were not elected to office and therefore still did not have an equal voice with men in making the laws of this country.

Most of the suffragists went back to their homes, considering their work done. It was to be another fifty years before the sound of feminism was heard again.

Back To The Cave

A fifty-year silence followed the first great feminist struggle to win the right to vote.

One reason was male backlash. "We gave you the vote," men said, "what more do you want!"

The men of the twenties understood that feminism was a threat to their centuries-old power over women, to their sense of entitlement for themselves, to their exploitation of all the environment (including women) for their personal use.

They may have been forced by the feminists to give women the vote. They even enjoyed some of the new personal freedoms women claimed: shorter skirts, drinking with their men in public, greater sexual freedom, young women around the office instead of male secretaries (now women served men outside the home as well as inside). From the south, black women were coming north to New York and Chicago to better themselves during the Great Migration and ended up as domestics. Because the men were not about to give up the real power, either politically or economically, that they had always held.

Another reason we got no further than winning the right to vote was women themselves. Political muscle is the only true guarantee of equality. Those women who remained active in politics made two enormous mistakes. They did not push for political office themselves, they supported male candidates. And while they continued to fight for human rights — for African Americans, for oppressed workers, for victims of Franco's Spain and Hitler's Germany, for child labor laws, for pure food and drug statutes — they stopped fighting for women's rights, considering them all won. They did not understand themselves politically. They thought they were free.

So instead of continuing the fight in the political arena, women reveled in their small, personal freedoms of dress and life style. The few feminists left were ridiculed, women's political consciousness was watered down. Having got the vote, they figured that was all there was to it, and they turned their attention to a personal search for fulfillment instead of laying the groundwork for political and social rights for all women everywhere.

Women had not yet come to realize that to win the battle for civil rights is one thing; to win the battle against prejudice is another.

Okay, we got the vote — but nobody would vote for a woman, not even many women.

Okay, we got jobs — but we got the worst jobs, the worst pay.

Okay, we got ourselves educated and into the professions, but those first women in business and the professions were thought to be freaks, just as the early feminists were thought to be holy terrors and man-eaters. The result was that a girl growing up had one of two images to choose from: she could either retreat into the narrow submissive-but-adored wife and mother role, collapsing back into their prisons like so many ex-cons do because they think they cannot make it in the outside world, or she could plow forward in her chosen field and risk becoming what everybody thought of career women — if not man-eater, women loveless and alone. Most black women had to work outside of the home without benefit of education or professional opportunity, but the domestic work they did mostly was not seen as unfeminine. There wasn't much of a choice, and many girls, understandably, did not see that there was a third choice — becoming a successful human being on all fronts.

Society helped women betray themselves. In the twenties, sexiness was the fashion, and "romance" became entangled with marriage. Many wanted to be a flapper, a sultry Theda Bara, an adorable Clara Bow, a beautiful and romantic Greta Garbo. The movie-and-magazine culture emphasized romantic marriage, personal style, and lured women away from their feminist solidarity with its emphasis on work and independence, back into marriage and housekeeping and bonding alone with a man. The image of marriage had been glamorized, the Myth of Emancipation was in the air, but the fact was, women's position in society was not much different from before. Trying to be a sexy movie star obviously wasn't the answer to women's happiness. Not that Ethel Waters or Bessie Smith, or Hattie McDonald or Butterfly McQueen, the great black actresses who just wanted decent roles instead of maid roles hadn't always been serious about their work. They set a serious example as actors and as working women.

In the thirties, the Depression sobered women as well as men. So instead of flappers, women began to be do-gooders. But they were still miserable, they still weren't fulfilled, and it began to confuse them. They had the vote, they didn't understand what more they needed, and secretly they began to wonder if they were inferior after all.

The early forties helped. With the men away at World War II, women filled many powerful positions and began to feel like human beings instead of second-class citizens. It's a sad commentary that it took a world war to give women a chance. Society genuinely needed women to work to their fullest capacities then, and for the first time many women were given human instead of "female" treatment.

And then two things happened. The men came home from the war to reclaim the jobs and fill the universities (men were still given preference in most places, of course). And the message of Freud and other *male* psychologists and scientists filled the air. Between the age-old prejudices against women as inferiors and the new prejudices formed by the new, still male science of psychology, women were slapped back down all over again.

In the late forties and fifties Freudian thought made a tremendous impact on the American woman. Because Freud was a genius, because he was the founder of psychoanalysis, because it was he who discovered the unconscious workings of the brain that influence our behavior, educated people everywhere accepted Freudian pronouncements as truth. No one can question the contribution Freud made to our pursuit of knowledge, to science, to man's understanding of himself. But that's exactly the problem. Freud helped *man to understand himself — he knew nothing whatever of the psychology of women.*

First of all, like most Victorian men, Freud believed a woman's place was in the home, and in the home only. (One would have hoped that Freud had known better, but he was alas a man, and a nineteenth century European man at that.) In letters he wrote to Martha, his fiancee, during the four years he made her wait before their marriage, Freud said:

> *"I know, after all, how sweet you are, how you can turn a house into a paradise, how you will share in my interests, how gay yet painstaking you will be. I will let you rule the house as much as you wish...."*

Freud spent years telling Martha to be a good little wife and devote her interests only and entirely to *him, his* house, *his* interests. He was convinced it was the only way any woman could be happy. In another letter, on the subject of John Stuart's views on "female emancipation," Freud wrote,

> *In his whole presentation, it never emerges that women are different beings....It is really a stillborn thought to send women into the struggle of existence exactly as man. If, for instance, I imagined my gentle sweet girl as a competitor, it would only end in my telling her, as I did seventeen months ago, that I am fond of her and that I implore her to withdraw from the strife into the calm, uncompetitive activity of my home....Long before the age at which a man can earn a position in society, Nature has determined woman's destiny through beauty, charm, and sweetness. Law and custom have much to give women that has been withheld from them, but the position of women will surely be what it is: in youth an adored darling and in mature years a loved wife.*

"Anatomy is destiny," said Freud. "Women are lesser human beings, childlike dolls; their bodies and minds fit them best for housework and the bearing of children and the service of men. Our ideal of womanhood would be lost, if women were educated to take their places in the world." (Not that Freud thought most women were fit to be educated anyway.)

(Don't forget, as you read this, that people *truly believed then and still do* what Freud had to say!)

Freud stressed the important influence that childhood had on a person's adult years. (It took Carl Jung, student and colleague, to discover that not only our personal, but our biological, species, and racial histories as well as personal histories were indelibly printed in our unconsciousness also.) But what Freud said was that mature mental health depended to a great extent on what had happened to a person as an infant and child. He was the first to discover that children are sexual beings from the beginning of their lives, and that their early sexual feelings determine a great part of their personalities later on. Freud's theories formed much of the basis of the field of psychology today, and though there are many more women psychologists than men now, it is still male theory that predominates.

In one area, however, he was not only wrong, but he did untold damage. That area was his theories on women. He conceived of an idea he called "penis envy." He believe that women themselves and all men considered females inferior because they don't have penises. He thought that women spent their whole lives wishing they had penises and feeling that people who had them were better than people who didn't. He said that when children discover that girls don't have penises, both boys and girls believe it is because somehow the little girl's penis has been cut off. As her vagina and womb aren't visible, both end up thinking of her not as a different but equally gifted child, but as a boy-with-something-missing, an inferior human being.

Feminist psychiatrists and many male psychiatrists know now that this is nonsense, that girls feel inferior because society treats them that way, not because they are without penises. After all, boys don't have uteruses, and they don't walk around feeling inferior because they can't produce babies. While it's true that many girls do envy boys or go through periods when they want to be boys, what they envy is not masculine sexual equipment, but masculine freedom.

Freud went on to say that because girls felt less well equipped then boys, they often grew up neurotic or with a "masculinity complex." In other words, they tried to be like men. He viewed any woman who wanted to work outside the home, who wanted to follow a profession, who went into business, not as a woman trying to fulfill herself as a person, but as a woman trying to be like a man, a woman pretending to have a penis.

The effect of Freudian thought was exactly what you might expect. For twenty years — and it still goes on — people reversed their attitudes toward the gains the feminists had made. They went back to thinking, as Freud told them, that women were inferior, that they belonged in the home, and that any woman who wanted a career was sick in the head because she was trying to be a man. The prejudice against women grew worse than ever.

Freud's followers, both male and female psychiatrists, didn't help matters at all. Helene Deutsch, Bruno Bettelheim, Erik Erikson, Joseph Reingold — great names in their field — held Freud's views, seeing women as breeders, to be fulfilled only through a husband and children.

Erik Erikson said 1964:

Much of a young woman's identity is already defined in her kind of attractiveness and in the selectivity of her search for the man. Mature, womanly fulfillment depends on the fact that a woman has an "inner space" destined to bear the off-spring of chosen men, and with it, a biological, psychological, and ethical commitment to take care of human infancy.

Bruno Bettelheim (1967):

...as much as women want to be good scientists and engineers, they want, first and foremost, to be womanly companions of men and to be mothers.

Joseph Reingold (1969)

...woman is nurturance...anatomy decrees the life of a woman. When women grow up without dread of their biological functions and without the subversion of feminist doctrine and therefore enter upon motherhood with a sense of fulfillment and altruistic sentiment, we shall attain the goal of a good life and a secure world in which to live.

Even Dr. Spock (1969):

Biologically and temperamentally, I believe, women were made to be concerned first and foremost with child care, husband care and home care.

It makes pretty horrible reading, doesn't it? The tyranni-
cal male psychologists of the world seem to have passed
sentence on women everywhere, condemning them to serve
men and their children forever (those male psychologists
must, of course, find it convenient to have their wives serve
them while they continue to do the important work of
thinking!)

Happily, the many great women in the Association of
Women in Psychology have begun to attack these views and
so end such stupid nonsense and such ignorance for all time.
And books like Gloria Steinem's best-seller *Revolution from
Within: A Book of Self-Esteem*, *Reviving Ophelia* by Mary Pipher,
and Peggy Orenstein's *SchoolGirls* are teaching mothers and
daughters everywhere to stop kneeling in the inferior position. (If the phrase 'self-esteem' boggles the mind as there
may not be much about our greedy, grabby selves to esteem,
substitute confidence, competence, the energy for life with
which we were all originally endowed.)

But the point is to stand up tall, and ignore the qualities
of childish passivity society wants to project onto us by flattering us into doing all the nurturing of everyone else or
preferring us as little girls instead of grown women. What
these women — and we here — are talking about is that our
standing tall is an inside job as well as a matter of law, a
matter of understanding our own worth whether anyone
else likes it or not.

(One result of keeping us childish and innocent, instead
of equal and responsible, is teenage pregnancy. It goes without saying that if we do not understand that teenage girls,

not just boys, are full of hormones and sexual desire, that many girls will be just as unable to say no at two o'clock in the morning as boys. And they will be equally unprepared with a condom.)

Women did not get much help from other sciences during the middle of this century either. American sociology, during this period, stressed the differing functions of men and women as opposed to the fact that we are all human beings with the right to grow and fulfill our lives. Sociologists talked of the division of labor as you-do-this-and-I-do-that instead of we all take turns. It was the era of the homemaker-breadwinner recipe for marriage.

In the excitement of discovery of new fossils and studies in the field of anthropology, the situation was no better. As Elaine Morgan points out in her book *The Descent of Woman*, evolutionists were so busy talking about mankind and about man as the hero of our history (called *history*, naturally, not *herstory*), that woman and her contributions to evolution were generally pretty much ignored. As Elaine Morgan says, half of our ancestors were women, which means that half the genes we have inherited belong to women, which further means that half of what men, as well as women, are is directly attributable to women.

It would be nice, as Elaine Morgan says, if just once we could read a volume that began, "When the first ancestor of the human race descended from the trees, she had not yet developed the mighty brain that was to distinguish her so sharply from all other species...."

Again, happily, there are now some paleoanthropologists who think of Lucy, a small, graceful 3.18-million-year-old partial *Australopithecus africanus* (just means southern ape of Africa) whose remains were discovered in 1974 in Ethiopia and who became the oldest and most complete hominid known — as the mother of humankind. Lucy stood upright and made the break to bipedalism, according to paleoanthropologist Mary Leakey and many others. It was certainly a female not unlike Lucy who stood up with her baby on her hip and who altered and enlarged the human brain with her hips to provide more efficiently for that baby!

But back to the cave. While it is perfectly true, then, that after the 1920's many American women had won a great many rights we had never had before, public opinion was still against us. There is not much point in teaching a girl to do algebra, letting her play baseball, letting her think independently, and giving her a college education if, at the end of all that, everybody says, "Go home and stay there. Or if you must work out of necessity, have the femininity to cringe at the bottom of the ladder." Voting and the right to an education are all very well, but if society and its scholars tell you that you're a second-class person, a man "with something missing," and that if you leave the house you will never really be fulfilled, it can really mess your head up.

It's as if girls were being told: "You can try to do what you want with your life, but if you do, you're a freak."

It was, it can still be, a damned-if-you-do, damned-if-you-don't situation.

The Beginning Of Success

The general attitudes of society, Freud included, made the fifties the worst decade for women since the winning of the vote. Betty Friedan documents it brilliantly in *The Feminine Mystique*. She calls it the great sellout of American women. *Good Housekeeping, Parents' Magazine, True Confessions* were the Bibles, and their message was that the only true and happy role for woman was the creative art of washing dishes and diapers. It wasn't described as one of the many possible choices for women — it was described as the *only* choice. And if you weren't happy scrubbing floors, you were some kind of sickie. What you got in return for the sadness of discovering that "romantic marriage" wasn't all it was cracked up to be were *respectability* and painkillers like Try a New Diet, Try a New Sewing Machine, Try a New Approach to Cooking — or, if you were really going out of your mind — Try a New Psychiatrist.

If the mothers of the fifties were lost and confused, young girls didn't fare much better. Nobody remembered that to feel like a free human being, you have to act like one. So young women, instead of taking a long, hard look at their mother's lives and trying to figure out a better way, escaped from their dull homes by following the same path their mothers had — Falling In Love. Only they did it earlier and earlier. What had been reserved for the late teens moved into the early teens. The Parked Car, The Parent-Empty House, Popularity In General, Being Adored In Particular. The Dating Ritual remained essential rites in the life of a girl. They just began earlier. And still the boys grew up to achieve; the girls, after a brief teenage fling, were sent back into the home. No matter how you didn't want to turn into your mother, you did.

By the sixties, the boys had had enough of the elongated romantic ritual. Freedom was in the air, what with the civil rights movement, the rise of the drug culture, the new music, the I Know What I Want And I Want It Now urgency that eventually gave birth to the Me Generation. Among the things the boys figured was that there had to be an easier way to get sex. There was. The boys began to leave home in hordes — for Europe, for the Peace Corps, for Greenwich Village, the riots of Berkeley, the civil rights demonstrations in Mississippi, the hippie scene from Haight-Ashbury to the

East Village to the ashrams of India, anywhere away from the controls of parents and a rigid society. And wherever they went, the boys found "cool chicks" to "swing" with. If the girls at home didn't want to play, they were called "up-tight" and shrugged off. There were plenty of "chicks" around who were still so anxious for male approval they would live any way the boys wanted them to live. The girls were still afraid to get together and made a stand, and each, in private, still searched for her own private solution.

One of the places in which girls and women began to do their own thing was in the area of radical politics, not yet on their own behalf, but, like the women of the thirties, on behalf of other causes. They were involved in the peace movement against the war in Vietnam. But more important for feminism, they were involved in the civil rights movement.

And just as the fight in the 1840's and 1850's for the abolition of slavery had spurred women to fight for their own freedom, so the fight in the 1960's against racism spurred a renewed battle against sexism. Women, feeling oppressed themselves, identified with all minority groups, and grew angry. And, for the first time in fifty years, they raised their voices and began to fight back.

But it was not just the civil rights movement that spurred women to fight for their own rights. Once the technology of the nineteenth century had matured into the advanced technology of the twentieth and had freed women of much hard drudgery through household machinery, and the birth-control devices of the twentieth century had allowed her to choose when she wanted to have a baby, the freedom of women was inevitable. It was simply a matter of time, and the time had come.

On August 26, 1970, thousands of women across the United States joined in parades, meetings, and demonstrations, to celebrate the fiftieth anniversary of the day women won the right to vote. Some of the slogans that day were funny: "Don't Cook Dinner — Starve a Rat Today!" and "Don't Iron While the Strike Is Hot!" But the aims of the National Women's Strike for Equality that day were serious. The women were demanding equality of jobs, pay, and education; free round-the-clock-child-care centers; free abortions for all women who want abortions; and the passage of the Equal Rights Amendment to the Constitution.

On that day, there were so many demonstrations across the country, and the women's movement had obviously become so widespread, that politicians everywhere began to realize that they had better take the movement seriously. That day marked a turning point in the history of women. They had emerged from the cave into the sunlight and meant to stay there.

There were many organized groups of women all over the United States who were fighting for women's rights that came out of that period.

NOW — the National Organization of Women — was begun in 1965 by Betty Friedan. It was the main women's rights organization on a national level. There were chapters throughout the country. NOW members fought on both national and local levels against sex discrimination in employment, housing, and education; they fought for twenty-four-hour-universal-child-care; and also worked to focus attention and gain support for the Equal Rights Amendment.

As NOW began to grow, other organizations began forming on a local level. Most were composed of women who were angry over job humiliations, who had suffered the horror of an illegal abortion, who were just plain miserable in their housewife roles. Many groups started simply as rap sessions designed to raise the consciousness of women socially and politically, to help them exchange views on their common troubles and problems. Many groups held demonstrations. In Atlantic City, they threw false eyelashes, padded bras, high-heeled shoes, and steno pads into a "freedom trash can" to demonstrate against the exploitation of women as represented by the Miss America pageant. (It was in Atlantic City that the myth of "bra-burners" began. In truth, feminists burned nothing at all.)

In New York City, feminists set up abortion referral services. *Ms.* magazine was founded by Gloria Steinem. In Boston, women picketed the Playboy Club. In Los Angeles, women broke into a CBS stockholders' meeting to protest the insulting image of women on the media. In Detroit, women dressed in black paraded past the city morgue to mourn dead sisters who were victims of illegal abortions.

All kinds of organizations sprang up everywhere. Federally Employed Women (FEW) was founded in 1968 to fight discrimination in federal employment. The Women's Equity Action League (WEAL) was founded as an association of professional women to focus on legal action. Women journalists organized, and at the 1970 convention of the National

Newspaper Guild, won support to end discrimination against women in press clubs and press boxes that had "male only" rules.

The National Association of Women Religious was organized in 1970 to protest their subservience to male priests and bishops. There are also hundreds of women's caucuses and committees in individual businesses, in plants, in sports, in the media. Women in science and engineering formed WISE. Wherever there are women, women are talking about and fighting for equal rights, equal practices, an end to harassment.

There are now resources and referral lists in organizations for teenage girls:

- **We Care for Youth**, P.O. Box 10399, Glendale, CA 91506 (818)279-3124 Focuses include getting and keeping girls out of gangs, job training

- **National Runaway Switchboard** (800) 621-4000. Represents over 1,000 agencies that serve runaways, homeless children, and other youth in high-risk situations and their families

- **Riot Grrls—Factsheet Five**, P.O. Box 17009, San Francisco, CA 94117. Guide featuring hundreds of zines (including *Grrls*)

- **New Chance (MDRC)**, 3 Park Ave. NY, NY 10016 (212) 532-3200. Provides services for young mothers and their children, lists of national educational programs

- **Lambda Youth Network**, PO Box 7911, Culver City, CA 90233. List of national and local resources for gay, lesbian, bisexual, transgender youth, AIDS education and information, P-FLAG chapters, variety of ethnic, professional, and cultural organizations (Send SASE and $1.00, include your age)

- See *Girl Power* by Hillary Carlip for more organizations and resources for all kinds of girls: Homegirls, Cowgirls, Farmgirls, Native American Girls, Rappers and Sistas, Surfers and Sk8ters, Jocks, Girls with Disabilities, Hotlines for Sexual Abuse

And read. People are recognizing everywhere the writings of women who are feminists or whose work makes comments on the nature of sexism: Virginia Woolf, Simone de Beauvoir, Doris Lessing, Anais Nin, Betty Friedan, Sylvia Plath, Kate Millet, Elaine Morgan, Gloria Steinem, Carolyn Heilbrun, Toni Morrison, Peggy Orenstein, Maya Angelou, Oprah Winphrey, McCorduck and Ramsey, Pipher, and many more. And read Alice Walker's *The Color Purple*, or at least rent the video. (Note: Alice Walker prefers the term "womanist.")

The long silence is ended. In America, and with the growth of the movement for women's rights in other countries, all over the world.

Section Three

WHAT YOU CAN
DO ABOUT IT

Think Straight

A lot of people still think of women's liberation and feminism as a great, big, nasty machine invented to gobble up nice, little girls and sweet, devoted housewives and rearrange them somehow into mannish monsters who grow moustaches and eat barbed wire for breakfast.

The fact is that feminism is a very simple idea: a woman can be a woman without being treated like a slave, an inferior, a possession, or a child. A liberated woman is a woman who thinks of herself as a *human* being as well as a sexual being; who thinks of herself as a person with her own interests and abilities, not as a sheep to be herded into whatever roles men (and her mother) choose for her. A liberated woman thinks of herself as an equal, not a side-kick. Above all, a liberated woman is a woman who believes she has the same right to *choose* what she will do with her life as a man does and to take the same responsibility for her life as a man does. (Remind your boyfriends, husbands, fathers, brothers, that what they get out of this is a friend, a buddy, who will share the fun, the burdens, and even the bills in life instead of being just a sexmate now and deadweight later).

To achieve this, we must come to think of all people as just that: people. The first step is to be *aware* of sexism, the division of people into male and female roles, in your own life experience.

Think about your early childhood. Were you given mostly dolls and dishes, while your brother or the boys in your neighborhood were given mostly cars, baseball bats, building blocks, toy guns to teach them to be killers? In kindergarten, were the boys mostly encouraged to play with the spaceships, the action figures, the dinosaurs, while you were plunked in front of the toy sink and plastic food?

Were you brought up to think in terms of being pretty? Was your brother brought up to think in terms of being pretty?

Were you given as much freedom to run around the neighborhood as your brother or other boys? (Why not? Bad things can happen to little boys just as well as to little girls. We are made to feel afraid for our bodies much too young. By the same token, when we grow up, it's the boys who are sent into the army to fight, never the girls. Why? Does the world really think a girl's body is more precious than a boy's?)

When you were in elementary school, were the girls and boys treated the same way? (They probably didn't behave the same way. Your memory of those years is probably that the boys were noisy and got punished more often, and the girls were quieter and got better marks. That's mostly because girls and boys are brought up differently at home.) But did the teachers make any effort to even things out? Did they encourage the girls to be more assertive? Did they encourage the boys to take pride in neatness or spelling marks? Did they help the girls increase their science and math skills and the boys toward better verbal and relationship skills? Did they, at school, try to even out the playing field? If you think back, the standards for girls and boys were different, weren't they?

And at home. What was it like at home? How old were you when you were given the feeling that marriage to the "right" man was the most, if not the only, important thing in a girl's life? (It's possible your mother hasn't mentioned *your* marriage yet, but how often do you hear her discuss other women's lives *only* in terms of their marriages? "Dora's life is awful because she's married to the wrong man." Should a marriage totally ruin a life? Or, "Yolanda must be miserable, she's never married and has no children." Why? Some women prefer not to get married and have children; they have other satisfactions: in their work, in their friends, in travel, in their own inner resources. A friend who is a biologist and another who is a business executive both say they get really tired of having people cluck at them sympathetically because they didn't marry. They both could have married. They simply didn't choose to. Another friend is a wild-life rehabilitator. She adores heron babies and swan babies and parrot babies and eagle babies — she has just no interest in human babies.

And did your parents and other parents you knew talk to little boys about love and marriage in the same way? Or did they feel that his personal development, his education, the beginning of his career should not be interrupted by too early a marriage.

And speaking of little boys, while they were deciding whether to be a basketball player, an astronaut, or a police chief, what were you deciding to be? If it was something more than somebody's mother or somebody's wife, was it a typically feminine, motherly career like teaching or nursing? (Both are excellent careers, but there is other work out there.) Many women are lawyers and doctors now, and many of the male professions in the sciences are open to women. But did it ever occur to you — or did anybody ever suggest to you — that you could do daring work, too? You could be a woman jockey like Kathy Kusner, who was the first. Like Linda Little Oklahoma, you could climb telephone poles as a linewoman, instead of being an operator. You could fight to be an airline pilot (United Airlines used to state openly that "pilots must be of the male species"), or go into the jungle to study wildlife, or drive a truck across country. And don't let them tell you it isn't womanly; you're a woman, so anything you do is womanly.

The point is, were you brought up as boys are to seriously believe that you could be anything you wanted to be from a stunt rider to a nuclear physicist. Or was it planted somewhere in the back of your mind by your parents, your teachers, counselors, or friends that in this world there are boy careers and girl careers, men's work and women's work, and that they are separate or different in kind.

Were you a "ladylike" little girl? Were you allowed to be as active and curious and get your knees as dirty and scraped as the boys? And if you were, were you called a "tomboy" — a way of saying "a girl doesn't need to explore and exercise her mind and muscles, but don't worry, she'll get over it and settle down nicely." (Why should an active girl be called an imitation boy?) It's true that there are lots of daddies today who cheer for their Little-Girl-Little-Leaguers. But how many of those daddies want to see this kind of activity in their little girls as they mature and become teenagers?

If you fell down and cried, what then? Were you held and comforted? Were the boys? Or were they told boys don't cry and to hold back their emotions while you were allowed to express yours. (The boys get the short end of it on this one! Men suffer a great deal because they are told to bottle up their softer, more tender feelings. And they make others suffer because they've only been allowed to express the emotion of anger as a "male" thing.)

Think about the differences now, in your teens. There must be hundreds of examples in your daily life that mark the separation of boys and girls into sex roles, that forbid girls to grow into equally mature and independent people.

In your school, despite the Title IX laws that mandate equal education, is there still gender inequity in which girls are given different courses from boys? In some schools, the system is really extreme, with the girls taking home economics, cooking, sewing, while the boys take machine shop, printing, mechanical drawing, computer repair, and other classes that lead to useful work in the outside world. (Not that kitchen duty isn't useful, but everybody, not just girls, should learn how to feed hungry faces.)

In other schools, there may not be such a division. But if there's no division of boys and girls in your school, is there a general feeling that boys do better in math and science and girls do better in the liberal arts? Are your career plans and work taken just as seriously as the boys'? What about the funds for sports? Do the girls' teams get as much sports training and equipment as the boys'? Or is it assumed that it is more important for the boys to play sports, and to know how to make a living than the girls. And if you are being encouraged to work, are you being encouraged to make a serious commitment to the kind of work you want to do for the rest of your life? Or are you being taught to think just in terms of a temporary job," just something to do until you get married." Or less meaningful work, or work at a less well-paid level in the work force?

Among African-American girls, because of the long history of women's strength and leadership in the home, with women often heads of households, often the only support, there is greater confidence. Studies have shown that because black girls are more confident about themselves and about their ability to work and help support their families, too often they want to prove their worth by quitting school too early to take a job. Many girls, of all backgrounds, ethnic groups, but especially girls with culturally distinctive, disadvantaged, or abusive backgrounds, and who are devalued by the educational system, drop out for low-paying jobs or motherhood. This is too temporary a boost to their sense of worth, however, and in the long run, destructive. Better to resist inside the system, get an education for better-paying, more satisfying work. Don't cut off your own legs to spite the world: it won't care.

And what about the books you read? Are they always about famous men? Have you ever been taught about famous women? I mean besides Betsey Ross (sewing), Florence Nightingale (nursing), and Queen Victoria (who had lots of babies and adored Prince Albert). Surely the history of the suffragists, and the struggle for women's rights, is as important as the history of all those men on horses in the Middle Ages. Surely Rosa Parks was as brave as Pancho Villa, Madame Curie as great a scientist as Jonas Salk. And after all, Jane Austen's novels are just as good as Charles Dickens's, and Mary Wollstonecraft's political writings just as important as any written by men.

It's a real put-down to be taught over and over again how great men are —and never to hear anything about the great work women have done.

When you think about your upbringing, both at home and at school, *both the open and the hidden agenda*, try an experiment. Try imagining, when you were born, that you had been born the other sex. Would your upbringing have been equally as suitable? If not, there was something wrong with your upbringing.

It is important to have this kind of awareness. Because life is hard. Most people never understand their upbringing, their conditioning. They arrive in adulthood thinking they're the only way they can be, mostly miserable, often short-changed, sometimes experiencing a little pleasure or satisfaction, always in conflict inwardly or outwardly from the moment they are born until they die. Because people do not understand their conditioning, their background, they can never be free of it. Be one of those who gets it — and gets free! Write a new script. Write your own script, don't just inherit one unthinkingly.

Think about the attitudes of the girls and boys you know. Do the boys talk mostly about sports, their work, what's going on in the world, about cars and machines, about sex and politics and technology, about who's selling what and who's going where — while girls talk mostly about boys, love and marriage, clothes and diets? Do the boys think in terms of themselves, while the girls think in terms of the boys? Why isn't everybody concerned equally about all these things?

Learning to be aware of sexism wherever you find it, wherever you see it, hear it, or experience it, is the first step toward freedom. In books, in school texts or novels, on television, in movies, in magazines, in the attitudes of your friends, your parents, teachers, advisors, the boys you date, and most of all, in yourself, you'll begin to react whenever girls are spoken of or treated as helpless, childish idiots.

After you've learned to scream instead of laugh every time some creep calls his women a "bimbo" — or, more generally speaking, after you've learned to be aware that society is not very fair to girls — think about whether you are always fair to yourself and other girls you know. Girls often betray themselves without knowing it — by siding with boys against other girls, by joining in laughter at jokes against women, by secretly feeling males are more important.

The brain has no genitalia. While it is true that scientists say there are some differences in male and female capacities when they are born, it's nothing that can't be educated into balance, and it doesn't make one sex's brain better or worse than the other. It is equally true that there are many more significant variations among people in general than because you're a boy or a girl. Examine your own attitude. Do you truly understand that boys are not born with better minds than girls? Or do you still feel instinctively that boys have better brains?

One of the problems in education is that we are taught outside knowledge (how to fling ourselves out into the universe and put a potty on the moon) but we are not taught about our inner workings: how the brain works, for instance. The brain has two basic functions: it observes, and it thinks. Thinking is all that memory stored, personal past, gender past, race and species past, yesterday, everything you've heard, learned, been taught. All that mental chatter you hear all the time in your head is thought. What you might like to do is observe all that thought. It's the best way to find out what you're thinking, is just to listen to your brain chatter away, listing all its lists, hearing the constant murmur of stress and distress, anxieties, fears, sorrows, pleasures, needs. *Everybody's brain does the same thing, all over the world, in Chinese or Arabic, French or Spanish, **male or female**.* Differences between people, cultures, sexes are there, but they are superficial. All human brains worry, are scared, are happy in the same way. And we all think all the time. *Observe this!*

"Feminine" and "masculine" are just words that describe what sex you happen to be, like "male" and "female." But do you feel somewhere inside you that there are basic feminine personality traits like self-sacrifice and submission and basic masculine traits like aggression and strength? Or do you understand that it's not males and females who are born so different, but all people who are born different. People have been brainwashed into thinking there are deep inborn differences between boys and girls that nothing can alter, when those differences are mostly a matter of training and of individual differences in people that occur regardless of sex. (An example is the widespread belief that women are born with better instincts for the care of children than men. There are too many wonderful brothers, male counselors, male teachers, male pediatricians, male social workers, to say nothing of the growing number of superb and caring fathers, to support such a belief any longer. The reason more mothers than fathers take over child care is simply that they have been told it is their function in life to do so.)

Make a list of all the traits you consider masculine, and all the traits you consider feminine. Do all the boys and girls you know fit neatly into those categories? If not, do you consider them peculiar? If a girl you knew wanted to be an architect, and a boy you knew wanted to be a nursery school teacher, would you think of the girl as "masculine" and the boy as "feminine?" Is there something wrong with a boy who loves cooking or a girl who loves racing cars? Or do you really believe that we are all human beings with the individual right to love, hate, and work at whatever we wish?

What about your own plans?

How do you feel about the traditional sex-role system? Do you take your work in school seriously? Are you aware of the sometimes different tracking systems for girls and boys (and, of course, if you are a young black woman or a woman of color, you may find that despite the laws, there is a color tracking system as well to further humiliate you: you know, the A classes full of white boys, the B classes full of white girls and boys, the C and D [crazy and dumb?] classes full of children and teenagers of color)? Do you plan a career? Do you think marriage is every girl's solution to life? If you're planning to marry someday, do you think the housework and the care of children should be shared so you don't end up feeling permanently caged with small wild animals? Or is all that a woman's responsibility? If you marry, will you go on working? Will your husband's interests always come before yours? Do you think you would be a failure, or unwomanly, if you didn't marry and have children? Do you think you would be a failure if you didn't have a career? Do you think you will need a man to "take care of you?" Or will you be able to take care of yourself and love a man as a free and independent person?

Do you think of lesbians as strange and outrageous? Or can you view them as equally worthwhile and caring human beings? If you are a lesbian, are you willing to take charge of your own life and be self-reliant and true to your own life wherever it leads?

If you are absolutely truthful with yourself, you may find some of your own answers surprising. You may be freer than you thought, or not so free after all. A lot of people are more prejudiced against themselves than they think and the way you think of yourself becomes, after a while, the way other people think of you.

Knowledge, second-hand from other people or just from books, is easy to come by. That's just intellect. But observation, the daily understanding of your life and how to live it rightly—that is true intelligence. Watch yourself, and the watching itself will change your life.

Krishnamurti, one of the greatest 20th century thinkers and philosophers, in a book called *The First and Last Freedom*, talks about the intelligence to watch and understand your programming so it doesn't get in your way. Instead of going off the cliff with the rest of the sheep or following someone else's tracks like a mule—you can be a light for yourself and go your own, right way.

What About Boys?

Girls in junior high schools and high schools across the country have begun to get together and talk about the feelings and problems they have as girls, examining themselves in the light of liberation, feminism, the future of women. In one discussion group held at a medium-sized, multicultural junior high school in a large city, these were some of the answers to questions I asked.

Madeleine: "I think the biggest problem girls have is boys. If you don't have a boyfriend, everybody thinks you're a failure. And if you do have a boyfriend, you have to change your whole personality around to keep him."

Dashelle: "If you have a different opinion, you don't dare argue back too much. Boys don't like girls to be brainy. But the bad part is, after you act dumb to please them, they think you really are dumb. It makes me sick."

Pam: "What I hate is, what's cool for a boy to do isn't cool for a girl to do. I mean, even if she's stronger, she has to pretend to be this silly, feminine person. I once watched a boy try to get a lid off a jar and a girl I knew who had a brown belt had to just stand there and watch him. But the worst is the sex stuff. They grab at you and call you "bitch" and "slut" and make you think all you are is a body to them. You feel really freaked out. But the worst is, there's nothing you can call them back that makes them feel as bad. And they'd just love to be grabbed!"

Deirdre: "What bothers me is not being able to call a boy up if you like him and want to see him. I grew up with a boy who was a very good friend. When we were younger, I could just call him up and say 'come on over.' When you're in your teens, you can't do that anymore. You can't just be friends. And if you call a boy for a date, everybody says you're chasing him."

Dashelle: "If you like a boy, all you can do is act sexy and wear sexy clothes. If you make one real move in his direction, you're gross."

Liz: "The boy I go out with never has any money. He gets nothing from his parents and his part-time delivery job has to pay for his clothes, his books, his carfare, everything. I get an allowance, and I'd be happy to pay for our dates. But he says it makes him feel bad if a girl pays, so we end up doing nothing. I don't see why it has to be that way, with the boy paying all the time."

Rita: "Once I liked a guy a lot, and he didn't call. After about three weeks, my mother suggested I give a party and use that as an excuse to call him up. I did it, but I really didn't like having play games like that. My mother said I better get used to it. You have to play games to get the boy you want. Even after you're married, the woman has to play games to get the man to do what she wants."

Dashelle: "I get so tired of worrying all the time whether I'm pretty and sexy enough. I remember going to my first party, and all I did for days ahead of time was worry about whether some boy would ask me to dance or whether I'd just end up standing around with other girls. I wonder how the boys would like it if they had to spend most of their lives worrying about whether they were handsome and sexy or if some girl was going to ask them to dance."

Liz: "Another problem with the boys paying for everything all the time is I always feel sort of as if they had bought me for the evening, so I have to do what they want and go where they want. If they do ask you, it makes you feel uncomfortable because you never know how much money they have. Sometimes I'll want an extra hamburger or I'll want to take a taxi instead of a bus, but you can't really ask them if they have enough money. I don't see why girls can't pay for things as well as boys. It would solve a lot of problems."

Pam: "One problem it would solve is the feeling you get when a boy has taken you out and spent money on you that you owe him what he wants afterwards. It's hard enough trying to find something in common to talk about to guys who only talk about sports and VCR's and CD players and computers. It's bad enough worrying about date rape and pregnancy, how you get AIDS, about drugs, about guns in the clubs you go to. But then you get to the big problem. If you make out with him because he spent all that money, you feel like a prostitute. Even if you make out with him because you like him, will he ruin your reputation by telling everyone?"

Dashelle: "And if you don't make out, will he ask you out again! You can get ruined if you don't let them do stuff, and you can get ruined if you do. You have to face the next day in school, and those boys' mouths can get real bad. They'll talk about your body right in front of you in the school hall."

Madeleine: "In school, a lot of girls don't raise their hands or answer questions right because they think it's unfeminine to sound too smart. Girls are always putting down their own intelligence in front of boys. And girls act silly and giggle when boys are around in a way they wouldn't do if they were just with other girls. I know, because I do it myself sometimes. It's degrading when you think about it afterward."

Liz: "For a long time, the boys in our class were calling all the girls "bimbo" and "who'" and "bitch" and worse. I wish television didn't have such a bad image of women. I wish gangsta rap would disappear for good. If the media didn't put us down and degrade us, maybe the boys wouldn't."

Rita: "Movies, too. We're always the sexy ones, while the man catches the criminals or whatever and maybe we help. And if we're not cooking for him, we're sacrificing everything for the man. In the teen magazines, it's always the feminine girl who gets the guy. Or if you look at *Vogue* or *Elle* or *Essence*, you really get an inferiority complex. You not only have to help, cook, sacrifice, and be feminine to get a guy, you have to be thin and fantastically gorgeous besides. Everywhere you look, you see something that emphasizes sex roles. The boys have to be successful and rich, the girls have to be beautiful and wussy."

Deirdre: "I think our worst problems is all we ever talk about or think about is boys. Listen to us right now! The way the boys behave is a big problem. But the biggest problem is ourselves. We're the ones who have to change. We have to think of ourselves as people who need what human beings need. We have to want to be somebody on our own, not just part of the life of some boy. And anyway, who says we have to get married at all! My aunt never married, and she's perfectly happy. She says she likes her privacy and coming and going when she pleases instead of when everyone else pleases. I know one thing; I'm not going to get married unless I want to. I'm not going to get married just because society says I should."

Rita: "I want to be a civil rights lawyer. I want to have a family, too. I just couldn't spend my life housekeeping the way my mother does. Even she agrees you get the feeling your whole life has been wasted if being a housewife is all you do. But when I tell my boyfriend I want to do both, he usually says I won't have time to do both, that if the wife is too busy with a career, who takes care of things at home. And when he found out that women with careers still only make about two-thirds of what men make doing the same thing, he wanted to know why I wanted to bother. Why not let him worry about the world, and I should just worry about him."

Pam: "My mother is a pediatrician. She's always worked, and she's always been a mother, too. She says men who still think a woman's place is in the home are prehistoric! I agree with what the women's liberation movement says, that both women and men should be able to do the work they want to do and that they should both have the fun of bringing up their children together. I think in a lot of families the men work so hard they never have time for their children. And if all the woman does is take care of her children, she gets too emotionally tied to them. If a woman works and shares the expenses, and a man shares bringing up the children, it gives everybody a chance to be a person and part of the family, too."

Madeleine: "I know a boy who once admitted to me that he was scared of having to be responsible for a wife and children, like what if he couldn't get a job or something. Maybe the sex-role system isn't fair to men either, making them responsible for earning all the money. I think maybe the boys get tired of having to be big and tough all the time, just the way we get tired of always having to be pretty and feminine."

Pam: "A boy said to me once, 'I get tired of always being the one who has to make the phone call. One day I was feeling bad, and it would have been nice if a girl had called me with a little sympathy for a change."

Dashelle: There's a boy in our class who doesn't fit the strong-arm male stereotype at all. He's quiet and gentle. He says he can always tell when his parents have had too much to drink, because his mother cries and wants him to take care of her and his father bullies him and asks why he isn't on the football team. What happens when he grows up? Does he have to support everybody in sight or get killed like a hero in order to prove he's a man?"

By the time the discussion was over, the girls had agreed on a number of points. Their first agreement was that girls should be treated at home and at school equally with boys. And since this was so, they felt they should also pay for things equally, partly so they wouldn't feel 'rented' for the evening, partly to keep things fair to both sexes. Decisions about everything from their dates to going together to their eventual shared lives, where to live, where to go, what to do, all decisions should be shared as well as expenses. This system would give girls more self-respect, and with more self-respect they might not worry so much about pleasing a boy by playing dumb and pretty to make him feel smarter and stronger. This might lead, the girls thought, to boys feeling less superior and entitled to everything. If they respected the girls more because the girls respected themselves more, there might be less sexual harassment. The girls agreed it was time to claim their due instead of waiting until it was handed to them — if they were lucky.

The girls also agreed they had to work together to help change the attitudes of teachers and their parents as well as the boys, instead of each girl out for herself. They knew they had a lot of tradition to fight, about dating, about male and female roles. They would have to let their teachers know it was important to call on them in class, to teach about women as well as men, so the boys would learn respect. They would have to ask their parents to get the boys to help with the laundry instead of always the girls, and to let girls have the same physical freedom as their brothers. They felt they had to turn the older generation around as well as themselves, or at least explain their position.

We said the factor of change is having an insight — an insight into something makes you change the way you look at your life and therefore your behavior and therefore the reactions of the people around you. The change may be that they'll work with you or against you or just go away, but if you change, *other people have to change or get out of your face!*

What About Work?

Do you ever talk to other girls and women who are interested in being responsible for their own freedom? Do you talk to them, not just about all the problems you are having now as a teenager, but about what kind of person you want to be, about what kind of work you want to do?

Girls and women all over the country are discovering that it's only by getting together with other women that we'll ever find out what kind of people we are and what kind of people we want to be. It's no longer possible to accept male value judgments about a woman's role. We have accepted their value judgments too long. We have trusted men to think things out, not other girls or women. There is a sisterhood among women now. We are at last learning to share with and trust each other.

Discussion groups, rap groups or consciousness-raising sessions, conferences and zines, Internet chat rooms, girlfriends getting together, talking to grown women who are cool, dialogue is springing up everywhere. In high schools, on college and university campuses, among young girls victimized by society's sexuality, divorce, fatherless homes, gangs, drug and alcohol addiction, eating disorders, discrimination in school, at home, in their jobs, as well as mature women who have found themselves trapped in female roles in their marriages or at work—across boundaries of race, class, age, sexuality, and ability, women are finally getting themselves together.

If you want to start a group yourself, read the section in activist Gloria Steinem's *A Book of Self-Esteem: Revolution From Within*. The local chapters of the National Organization for Women, the YWCA, Riot Girrls zines, your own ad in a local paper—anything can help you organize what Steinem calls 'revolutionary groups' until there is what she calls a "national honeycomb of small personal/political groups committed to each member's welfare through both inner and outer change." As she says, if two white male alcoholics could start a national network of Twelve-Step programs that are free, leaderless, and easy to find, so can women of any age, any color, anywhere.

A man once asked me why it was necessary for women to organize talk groups. The explanation is that while men always had someplace to get together every day and be themselves—at the office, in bars, in sport groups, in clubs—women were isolated in their houses, isolated from each other. Even girls are often isolated, because when they are together they tend to be competitive over boys rather than supportive of each other. When I said this at a high school meeting once, a girl burst into tears and answered, "I always thought there must be something wrong with me because I felt alone. I didn't realize other girls felt they had no one to talk to."

There is somebody else who understands. The girl sitting next to you in class, other girls on the next farm, ranch, skate, or surfboard, in your gang, on your sports team, on your block, the woman sitting next to you on the bus or the subway, the saleswoman in the store, a woman teacher at school, and, believe it or not, your mother. They may not agree with you about your solutions to problems, they may not understand all the problems you face in a world more radical, more violent, with more guns and drugs and earlier sex problems than they faced, they may even be on the defensive about women's liberation (if they have not been free themselves), but they understand. They know what it means to be a woman.

Remind each other that *nothing is written in cement*. Examine the rituals you have inherited, the male-centered beliefs in a male god, a male-headed family, Freudian views, male-leadered hierarchies. All of these have only existed for a few out of the tens of thousands of years the human race has been around. And they are not necessarily either worthy or valid. A good example of not-necessarily-valid ideas is evolutionary progress. Many important 20th- century minds agree with the biologist Stephen Jay Gould who says:

> *"Progress is a noxious, culturally embedded, untenable, nonoperational, intractable idea that must be replaced if we wish to understand the pattern of history."*

This may be true of many of our beliefs, values, and rituals, not just the idea of progress. Many important thinkers of this century have discovered there is cause-and-effect, but no such thing anyway as progress, evolutionary, spiritual, or otherwise. Yet all of this is your birthright.

Be careful with your insights, however. Intelligence and perception are capacities unevenly distributed in families. Your friends and families *may not be able to see all that you see.* They need not be called wrong, but they may be limited. Don't inherit someone else's reality. Don't be satisfied with the way things are. Test everything out for yourself and talk it over with someone else. Also, remember that *only 15% of your information is with you at birth; 85% of your maturing happens afterward.*

If you can't change your genetics (yet), you can certainly change your experience.

As to practicalities.

Do you, when you think about the kind of work you want to do, let yourself consider all the fields that should be available? Do you believe you can do what you want to do? If the problem is job opportunity, there are legal ways to fight back, and women's groups already in place to help support you in your fight for the job you want, for equal pay, for maternity leave, for benefits. It is up to you, on a daily basis, to live so that you do not tolerate promotion discrimination, attitude discrimination, sexual harassment. *Do not let things that disturb you go by.* Organize women's groups, girls groups, female networks, and take action together.

If there isn't a group in your particular town or company, you can start one. For advice about sex discrimination at school or at work, for advice on how to set up groups, what and how to discuss, what and how to take action, check out Carol Kleiman's *Women's Networks* which describes women's support, self-help, and networking groups. Here is a group you can contact. The central organization will answer your letters and will refer you to a local chapter for guidance. Ask for their "NOW Guidelines for Feminist Consciousness-Raising," 1982.

National Organization for Women
1000 16th Street N.W., Suite 700
Washington, DC 20036
(202)331-0066

I mention this and other organizations in the book, because the likelihood of your getting good guidance at school is problematical. As you know, it's one thing to decide on a job or a career, for equal work and against discrimination, and another to find the proper guidance and the opportunity to go through with your plans. At home and at school, you may find that people say one thing, think another, and do an entirely different third thing. Girls have always suffered from lack of support.

Besides the lack of good advice and good support, even if you can get good training and equal admission into advanced education now, there is something else many girls lack because of early conditioning—what the world is currently calling self-esteem. Girls suffer from a lack of faith in themselves and in each other. Experiments have showed that when the same lecture was given by a female teacher and a male teacher, women college students rated the male "better." When a group of high-school students were asked whether they would vote for a woman president, many of them answered that they felt a man could do a "better" job.

When I met with a group of black female high-school students who were involved with the black activism at their school, most of the girls agreed that the boys knew more about politics. One girl said, however, "I get so sick of going out for sodas and sandwiches, sitting at the computer doing the letters and the database and the printing out. The guys say it's up to them to do the thinking, and up to us to help them by running the machinery. What I say is, it's hard enough to be put down because I'm black without being put down because I'm a woman, too. No point in having freedom for half a race."

Most working girls and women, even young ones, have permitted their roles to be defined by everyone but themselves. (People — mostly men, but not always—are forever saying things like "women are happier serving men," "women are happier when men take charge," "women are happier when someone else does the thinking for them."

Among many women, phrases like that cause a terrible grinding of the teeth!) Most women are aware that they are just as capable as the men they work with, sometimes even more capable. But they simply do not reach for the rewards their capacities entitle them to or even for ordinary equality. A woman I met who has worked for the same company for ten years knows how the firm should be run better than anyone else. She has trained a dozen or more young men to fill the position just above her own. It's idiotic! I asked her why she didn't request the job herself. Her answer was a slight shrug, half a smile, and the words, "What do you expect? I'm only a woman."

The women I know who have "made it" are generally those who expect to be treated as an equal. Many successful women are only children, or the oldest girl, or at least have been treated as sons by their fathers, often expected to carry on the family honor. And sometimes, they don't get as far as men with the same capacity (that glass ceiling!), without trying harder and fighting for what they want. But if they've done it, so can the rest of us. Remember, there are women now in almost every field, not just the professions and the sciences.

Even the crafts that require apprenticeship training and were once traditionally closed to women, the machinists, electricians, carpenters, plumbers, auto mechanics, now allow women in. There are women learning to be laboratory technicians, aircraft builders, shoemakers, construction workers, watchmakers, and skilled workers of other kinds. They are earning twice or more the salaries they would have earned as secretaries, waiters, cleaning personnel. So when you're thinking about the kind of work you want to do, know that there isn't anything you can't do as well as a man and maybe better. (I mention these crafts and skills especially in answer to the protest I've sometimes heard that the women's revolution seems to be geared toward those women who want to be doctors, lawyers, or astrophysicists. One girl wailed at me not long ago, "I've never gotten a mark higher than C in my life. All I'm fit for is to be somebody's stenographer." As it turned out, she happened to be pretty good with her hands, and when I mentioned carpentry among other possibilities, her face lit up. It just hadn't occurred to her that women were "allowed" that kind of trade.)

All of which is to say that the myths about women who work are being exploded: the myth that women are not as creative as men; the idea that women in government, in industry, and offices should have the jobs that are closest to housekeeping and a wife's duties (if we're not careful, we may end up being as tied to the computer as we once were to typing letters, the shopping, the family or office bookkeeping, as all that can be done on computer now); the myth that women actually prefer helping a man "do his thing" and only wanted to feel needed; and the myth that any woman who does big jobs, thinks for herself, and is successful must either be a nasty bitch or be sleeping with the man who helped her to the top.

These are ridiculous man-made myths. Up until now most people have accepted them, however, as truth—which is why so many women have accepted low-paying jobs and dead-end positions. That these myths have lasted so long is due to prejudice on the part of men and a sense of inferiority on the part of women.

Inferiority feelings may also account for some of the volunteer work women do. Giving some time for the good of the community is something all people should do, men as well as women, and do it as a natural thing to do to help the next fellow. In this country, we have a tradition of volunteering, not just for groups such as the League of Women Voters and the PTA, but to aid the poor and homeless, to serve as members of town boards and commissions, to be literacy volunteers, to name only a few.

But the housewife who does no paid work and devotes all of her time to volunteer activities does so because she has the secret feeling that, though she may want to work, she isn't worth much. Or if she does paid work, she loses her entitlement to being taken care of. Volunteer work gives women the feeling they are needed, but not that their work has a value. Just as women in families fall into the trap of supporting and encouraging everybody's needs but their own, just as women go into the "helping" professions, just as the feminists of the past ended up fighting for everybody's right but their own, women also go into the community to help everybody but themselves. Women have been saddled with being the tender and compassionate members of society whose primary purpose is to answer the telephone whenever anyone else puts in an emotional call. We answer the call because we have been trained to enjoy feeling "needed."

But the time has come to let the other half of the human race share the pleasure of being needed, while we share the pleasure of being *valued* and *paid*! (If you want to go into a service vocation, by all means plan to do so, but get a degree or at least some training—you'll be worth a lot more to society and you'll find your work a lot more satisfying, if you know what you're doing.) Even if you're a giver, you'll need to make some money if you want money to give away.

There is another pitfall girls sometimes encounter when they begin to plan their lives and careers, and that is deciding to do the kind of work you can do at home. The picture of the happy housewife painting, sculpting, or writing away with the children climbing around her knees is a pleasant picture—but a nearly impossible one. Creative work requires privacy.

It takes a great deal of discipline for a man or a woman to work at home. But if a man works at home, his wife keeps the kids strictly out of his way. Unless you are rich enough to have a housekeeper or sensible enough to find a husband who is willing to take over for several hours a day, or unless you plan not to have children at all—be aware that young children and work at home do not mix well. A nine-to-five job, with a clear-cut barrier between professional work and housework, requires much less discipline. By working at home, a woman risks turning into the family ogre by screaming for time and privacy; she risks losing her sanity from the constant interruptions of household affairs; and she risks getting so little done that she ends up earning very little or letting her career slip away entirely. (When my own children were babies, I risked those things daily. I made it through because I had a husband who took over for a few hours a day and stood faithful guard at my door. A close friend of mine who is a painter was less fortunate. Her husband traveled a good deal on business. She finally had to rent studio space away from her home in order to get any work done at all.)

More than ever before, women are breaking through the work barriers set up by men. Women are learning to esteem themselves more highly. Women are earning higher salaries and high positions. We finally have the first woman president in 150 years of the AMA, the American Medical Association in which only 11% are women while 20% of U.S. doctors are women. From 1987-1996, firms owned by women of color logged triple the growth rate of U.S. businesses overall, according to a report by the National Foundation for Women Business Owners and IBM.

This is because women have at last learned to talk to each other, to discuss their common problems, to compare their solutions, to stand together and fight together for their lives against domestic violence which can mean soul battering as well as physical battering.

It's hard to go it alone. But if you are a person who respects herself as someone with the right to be fully human, and if you are brave (and you will need to be brave, because there are still a lot of people around to hassle you for not getting a thrill out of the idea of being a household slave), understand that there are a lot of us around now willing and able to come to your support. If you need help, holler.

What About Marriage?

Marriage can begin in a lot of different ways at many different stages of a person's life. Just as boys are prodded early to think in terms of making a living, girls are prodded to think in terms of making a nest. It is rarely suggested to a girl that she need not marry, that marriage is just one of the possible choices. Mostly, girls are convinced, and convinced young, that in marriage lies the most important part of their future.

And unless you have significantly enlightened parents, it will not be suggested that:

1) if you are a lesbian you marry a woman

2) happily ever after may include merely one, or one husband after another (after all, when people invented the marriage vows, as Margaret Mead points out, humans rarely lived past 40 or 50 years old) — we now live 30 years longer in many parts of the world which leads to people changing goals, changing characters, changing partners

3) as women can now be self-supporting, you can marry whoever you like, and it is no longer necessary to marry for financial, family, class, race, religious security, strength, and social approval

4) if you have made a mistake, you can get a divorce

5) you can have children without a husband: family, friends, male and female, can be a child's extended parents, caregivers, role models

Too many girls are convinced too early in their lives that the only escape from home, the only way to set up an independent household, the only way to cope with the frightening big world out there is to get married. Sometimes just sex leads them into marriage. Girls who are taught they are worthless, incapable creatures respond to a hug. A hug, a flattering attention, a ride in a car, a compliment—and they can feel beautiful and loved for half an hour. Or at least desired. Or at least in command of someone's full attention. (Why is their pregnancy a shock? Why aren't the boys investigated and found equally responsible?) It is easy, when you are young, to confuse sex with love, especially when in our society fathers so often either leave or are emotionally unavailable that many girls are willing to accept this pattern of male abandonment.

Here are a few samples of the ways in which various marriages may happen:

ample Marriage Number One begins in the sixth grade. She has been brought up in a household where everybody keeps strictly to traditional sex roles. Under her mother's eye, she has learned how to cook, sew on her brother's buttons, launder her father's socks (cute, wifely little thing, isn't she?), and stay clean and out of trouble (the kind of trouble caused by being curious enough about something to want to take it apart, to run somewhere different and explore it, to climb on it, jump over it, or make a mess with it). She has learned how to get what she wants by flattering men, not earning things herself. She has learned to be "adorable," not direct. She has learned that it isn't necessary to "bother her pretty little head" with thinking, because men will always do that for her not only at home but at the office, in the voting booth, at the bank. She has understood that while it's true women do all the dirty work, there are two rewards for that: the first is that she will always be taken care of; the second is that she can have the fun of being a martyr. She will always do the thankless jobs. She will always be scapegoated—if the children are in trouble, it's her fault for not being a good mother; if the husband is unfaithful, she will have failed at being a good wife; if her mother complains, she will have been a bad daughter—but she can clutch her chest and sigh along with all the other scapegoats.

She has learned that the man is the center of all creation, certainly the magic center of a woman's life, and that without one, a woman is nothing. She has been told to pay no attention to the workings of politics, industry, the arts, sciences, or the rest of the great big world out there (clearly men's business except for a few pushy women), because the greatest act of creativity is having a baby (her business). She may even be taught to feel that this makes her better than a man. It's the "hand-that-rocks-the-cradle-and-winds-a-man-around-her-finger" syndrome (an untrue myth told by men and repeated by mother to daughter to make women happy believing they have a power that they, in fact, do not have at all). She grows up believing, however, that her only way to power and status is by serving a man, by making him dependent on her. He will take care of her, and she will share his status and his glory .

With all this in mind, she has been playing house since the day she was first able to hold a doll. "You be the daddy, I'll be the mommy," has always been her favorite game.

She plays the game for real the minute she can get a boy to respond. This can be as early as the fifth or sixth grade, what with girls maturing so much younger than ever. She singles out the boy who seems most willing to be flattered by her adoration (often a boy as emotionally dependent and unadventurous as she) and clamps on tight. She will follow him anywhere, do whatever he wishes. And because she has been trained so early in the feminine arts, she will keep his attention. She may have to try two or three boys in the beginning, but she will find one early in her life, keep him, and marry him. She will have to. Her entire life and sense of worth depends on it.

Her future? She will go on following him anywhere. Anywhere his company moves him, she will uproot her life and follow him, leaving friends, home, subordinating everything to his interests, his career. She will live in constant anxiety over whether he still loves her—she will diet, buy face creams, and spend hours in beauty parlors. Having no life experience or thoughts of her own, she will know, as they get older, that she bores him. She can turn to her children for comfort, but they will grow up and leave home. Her nest is empty, her marriage is empty. There is nothing left but her martyrdom, and her kitchen floor, both of which she shined up yesterday, shined up today, and will shine up tomorrow.

S*ample Marriage Number Two* begins during the middle of the teenage years. She believes in love, in romantic love. She, too, has been brought up in a house where everybody lives according to traditional sex roles. Only in this case, her parents' marriage is actively unhappy. Instead of exploring why an unequal marriage leads to frustration, alcoholism, abuse, infidelity, her mother explains the bad marriage simply by saying she married the wrong man. Her mother often talks about past men in her life and wonders how it would have been if she had married differently. This one would have earned more money; that one would have had a more important position; another would never have been unfaithful (thus causing her to drink), would have been more glamorous (thus not necessitating drink), would not have bored her to death (thus not making alcohol and pills her only escape from depression). It never occurs to the mother to teach her daughter to create a life for herself—all life comes through a man, the right man. In return for what the man does, a girl must be pretty, sexy, and charming at all times. The daughter is taught to be bewitching early in her teens, and she gets approval, not for work she has done well, but for the extent of her popularity with boys. Because of her parents' unhappy marriage and the constant misery at home, the girl's one idea is to escape and escape fast. She has not been taught to work or to earn her own way, even if she's had jobs to pay for her own clothes or schoolbooks. She has been taught that True Love with Mr. Right is the only answer to her happiness. So the obvious solution is to fall in love (or even with the idea of love) and get married —quick! Which she does.

Because she believes in Romance and has no true conception of what adult love means—chemistry, of course, but also shared interests, mutual respect, wanting the same things out of life, the excitement of knowing another person really well, a sense of responsibility—her marriage gets stale in a very short time. After all, it's not very romantic to clean house while your husband works and then comes home tired. She may take a job (it won't be an interesting one because she hasn't got herself trained to do much) or decide to have children (which is one of life's great joys but hardly romantic). In either case, she finds out after a few years that her world is no longer the picture of True Love she had envisioned. Like her mother before her, she does not understand that a woman has to fill her own emptiness herself, that no man can do it for her. Instead, as her mother did, she will blame her unhappiness on her choice of husband. She has three ways to go from there to recapture the romance and the fun she misses: she can take a lover; she can get a divorce and try again; or she can make a career out of her misery as her mother did.

S*ample Marriage Number Three* begins in the late teens after high school. She has been encouraged to use her mind some. Her mother may work now, or may have worked in the past, not because she enjoyed it, but to "help out" with the family budget. She has been told that she will have to "help out" with a job until she gets married, and that she may even have to "help out" with a job if her husband doesn't earn enough after she gets married. But she will not be allowed to think that any work she can do will be really worthwhile or that she can earn a great deal.

Work in this case is not meant to fill her with pride or result from special interests or give her a feeling of accomplishment and independence. Most likely she will take any job she can get and quit with a sigh of relief the minute she finds someone to marry or at least as soon as the man can support the family. "Whoever earns the money" in her life will always be the one whose decisions must be respected.

If she stays home to care for the house, the children, the garden, the finances, the cooking, the laundry, and works a seven-to-ten-o'clock schedule, this still won't make her equal with her husband in her own eyes because she isn't earning a salary for the work. Because she has worked and has acquired a little of the sense of self-reliance earning money gives you, she will respect this in her husband and lose respect for herself. On the other hand, the work she did was dull, she had no personal ambition to seek promotion, and she will use "who'll take care of the home?" as excuses not to go back to a boring job, unless money is desperately needed. In guilty return for the fact that her husband faces what she believes to be the boring work of the world every day of his life, she will bring him his TV dinner and his remote control to the day he stops drawing breath. Money should never equal power in a family, but for her it always will.

S*ample Marriage Number Four* begins in college or shortly thereafter. She comes from a family where education is given great importance, where girls are encouraged to do as well in school as boys. In her teens her parents applaud her good marks far more than the number of dates she has. At home she hears her father respectfully listen to her mother's opinions and sees him help out with the dishes and other housework. Because her parents respect each other too much to discuss problems in front of the children, their daughter may never inquire too closely into the workings of the marriage. (For instance, the fact that the father helps out with *her* dishes, *her* laundry, *her* kitchen floor, takes out *her* garbage—why isn't it their dishes, their laundry, their kitchen floor, their garbage!) Her mother may have a career, but it is clearly also her mother's responsibility to run the house. Nobody questions the fact that the mother has to assume two sets of responsibilities, career and marriage, while the father is really responsible—despite his help with the house and child care—only for his own career.

So although the girl is brought up to take her schoolwork seriously and to think in terms of an interesting career, she is still given to understand that in marriage, the man's work comes first. She is given to understand something else, too, although it is very little mentioned during her growing years. *She is expected to get married,* if not sooner, later, and have children so her parents can be grandparents (and in the usual way, please—not two lesbians adopting a child, not children of a single parent adopted or otherwise, not as part of a commune that adopts special needs children). This priority becomes apparent when she sets out for college or university, at which time she discovers from her parents that she has been sent only partly to get an education and only partly to prepare for the work of the world. She will have a career, of course, but she has also been sent to college to find a really first-class husband; her own education will fit her out to be the kind of wife an educated and successful man needs. The emphasis has suddenly shifted from her becoming a fully developed, independent person to becoming a first-rate wife.

It is girls like this one, the ones who have been educated to use their minds and their abilities and who then have to sink to second place in the household career scene—or even have to give up their work if their husbands' companies uproot them or if they live a "company" or "suburban" life that requires a lot of entertaining or playing "lady" at luncheons or in volunteer groups to advance their husbands' careers—who end up as alcoholics, on pills, or in psychotherapy. The frustration of giving up the pursuits of a well-educated mind, or the guilt and anxiety produced by having a career and also being totally responsible for the home (you can get the feeling you're not doing either as well as you should, especially if there are young children you have to leave in day-care every day in order to work) can be very difficult to bear. (It's still better, however, to bear both responsibilities and work the double-shift of job/children-and-home if necessary than to have no meaningful, or at least paid-your-own-money-so-you're-not-scared-and-dependent, work of your own—if the anxiety rate is higher, there is also pleasure, pride, and freedom to make up for it.) There is no more frustrated person in the world than an educated woman who exchanges a major in industrial engineering for diapers. (This is why male chauvinists will say, "It's a mistake to educate women at all.") The answer obviously is not less training of the mind, but more training in confidence and the ability to understand what is and what is not a full, right, and healthy life. Heilbrun talks a lot about our lack of female role models. Lacking them, she suggests using successful male role models instead, in making decisions about whether to remain at home or be part of the world.

Sample Marriage Number Five begins at any age with any girl who does not think of herself first and foremost as someone who has to get married to be a person. She thinks of herself as a full human being, free to make any and all choices. She will make the best use of her education and training. She will take her pick of any field or career, any trade that appeals or is available to her and suits her talents. If she finds doors closed to her, she will not accept the fact meekly. She will bang the doors open, not by wearing a tighter sweater, but by using her mind, her determination, her own strength and the organized strength of her sisters in a direct and open way as befits dignified people.

What is important to her in her relationships with a man is not the status and security an engagement ring is supposed to give, but a relationship that is founded on equality instead of dependence. When she marries, if she marries, they will both work, they will both share the housework of their household. If there are to be children (and there is no reason in the world why just because they can have children they *must* have them—in this overpopulated world there are no sociological or economic reasons arguing for the necessity of children in most countries) they will share the responsibility for bring them up.

They will not believe the myth that just because a woman carries a child she is best suited to nurture it. They will understand, instead, that both men and women can be nurturing and supportive, and that both men and women can be assertive and independent. They do not think that it is the man's responsibility alone to support the family any more than they believe it is the woman's responsibility to do all the cooking. If she needs more education, he will work. If he needs more education, she will work. They may both work part time, tend house and children part time. If a move becomes necessary to either career, both careers will be given equal weight in the discussion regardless of who is earning more money. They will live together as two free and independent human beings who choose to share their lives—not as "feminine" and "masculine" types shackled together for society's approval. In freeing herself to be what she needs to be, she knows she is freeing him as well to live as he wants to live. (Freedom doesn't mean, she realizes, doing anything irresponsible you please.) She will not expect him to be a big, strong man twenty-four hours a day, nor will he think of her as his darling nincompoop. They will both be strong when necessary, and both will have the right to lean a little when necessary. A girl may even elect to follow the traditional house-wife-mother role, but she knows that she does it of her own free choice and knows that eventually men will also be free to elect the house-husband-father role if they choose. No marriage is ever guaranteed. But an equal marriage, an unpossessive, unclinging, undependent, marriage full of fresh air for all to breathe deeply stands the best chance of making both partners happy.

S*ample Number Six* is no marriage at all. Or an arrangement where marriage or partnering without a legal marriage certificate occurs only AFTER the woman's career is on track and is not, after all, her main goal in life.

Certainly you do not have to decide as a teenager whether you do or do not want to get married. But it isn't too early to think about how you regard yourself as a person and how you relate to the boys you date. If you consider the kinds of marriages discussed in this chapter, you may find some traits you recognize in yourself, your friends, your parents. You may find you want to change some of the patterns you've been following, or you may be satisfied right now with the way you feel. Part of the problem of being a teenager is, there you are, in a maelstrom resembling a psychotic episode, or a wild storm of hormones, being scared to grow up and scared to stay a child, scared of the world and not wanting to stay home, if you have a home; wanting friends and their approval (what do you have to trade for this, do you have to have sex, do drugs, join gangs, starve, mutilate yourself, lie, die?)— there you are, lonely and half crazy in a whirlwind, with no experience, no money, no solid ground under your feet—and you are asked to begin to make the most important decisions of your life: about work, about marriage, about children.

At least give yourselves a break and understand you are as free, if you let yourself be, as any boy in your family or class or neighborhood, rich or poor, black or white, gay or straight, fat or thin, to choose what you will do with your life and that you are entitled to exactly the same right to fulfill your needs as he is. That is the whole point of the women's revolution.

The Fight For Your Own Survival

I have heard many girls and women say that coming upon the reality of a women's revolution is like walking out of a small, dark room into the sun. To realize that other women and girls feel constricted by the roles normally given to women, to know that women everywhere are tired of the limiting roles of sex object, goddess (not much room to move on top of a pedestal), mother, wife, dependent, servant, to understand that it's not just you, but all women, who are tired of feeling that it's a handicap to be born female—to be aware of these things brings an incredible measure of relief.

Liberation is based first on insight into your lack of freedom, then on personal courage. It begins with the knowledge that you need never take second place to a man. It means that you do not have to choose between femininity and achievement—you can have both. It means that you can choose marriage, children, and a career (as men always have), instead of having to give up one part of your life for another. It means that you need not marry and have children at all, or if you do, that you can marry a man who believes in equal sharing or that you can make use of day-care centers (or cooperative baby-sitting arrangements) for your children. Liberation is knowing you have the right to be a housewife, an astronaut, or both, and that you will fight for that right if necessary. It is a deep understanding that being a big-haired mall bunny is not a recognizable ambition.

Liberation is also a willingness to discuss publicly what you know to be so. You don't have to be a political activist, but you do have to live politically right—meaning fairly, morally, with consideration for all, including yourself—and the understanding that right action is based on the good of the many, not just the self. This isn't "idealistic," it's practical: if everyone isn't all right, sooner or later you won't be safe either. You won't get far by having the secret feeling you're an equal human being—and then not answering a question in class because the boys might not approve of an intelligent girl. Nor will it help you much to know you can do a job perfectly well and then to take less money for it than they would pay a man. There's not much point in getting annoyed over women being treated as sex objects, and using a good pair of legs to get yourself a job, or a promotion, or a raise. There's damage for all girls if you join in blaming a young girl or a woman for being raped. It's like blaming the poor for being poor, the disadvantaged for their lack of advantages. It is not only stupid, it is mean-spirited. If you get through life not being among the majority of women who get short-changed, stalked, harassed, or raped, that means you are lucky, not a better person.

It won't help to grumble about being tracked into sewing, cooking, and home-economics classes in school unless you're willing to struggle with the administration to change the tracking system so that both boys and girls can take cooking and/or machine shop. In social situations, you can't really believe in yourself as a girl if you laugh at or pass off anti-women jokes and smutty remarks. This doesn't mean you shouldn't have a sense of humor, but truly derogatory remarks are seldom really funny. When you betray yourself in any of these ways, you are also betraying other girls and women. And conversely, when you win in any given situation, you've won not only for yourself, but for the next girl who comes along.

Groups of women are fighting many public battles today—for equal pay and job opportunities, for the right of every woman to decide whether she wants to continue a pregnancy or not (remember the absolute requirement for birth control, based partly on the insecure status of abortion rights), for the right to equal education, for fairer property

and divorce laws, for an end to the ridiculous and demean-
ing image of women in the media—television, commercials,
ads, books, movies — for federal funds for child-care centers, to elect both male and female legislators who will pro-
mote the cause of women's rights, and above all, to put an
end to thousands of years of discrimination against women
politically, legally, and culturally. Women everywhere are
working to reeducate the public by appearing on television
and radio, by holding conferences, by writing books, by dem-
onstrating and picketing. And to an even greater extent they
are doing it by long conversations everywhere they go—in
laundromats and supermarkets, over cups of coffee and the
heads of their playing children, in diners and offices, in factories, in schools—wherever two or more women get together these days, they talk.

Many of your mothers might have been or still are in the
women's movement, and they understand. Do not listen to
those people tell you things used to be better: while it is true
there is more violence, there is no longer legal slavery or
legal racial segregation (though servitude and racism are
alive and well); while there is more noticeable child abuse,
incest, rape, and sexual harassment, women can now vote
to make certain it is noticed; while there is still condoned
murder in the form of war, there is less condoned personal
revenge allowed to pass. Yes, we have more drugs, more
drug-related crime, yes, there is more visible teenage pregnancy, yes, we are ruining natural environments and reduc-
ing natural habitat—but also, and perhaps for the first time

in known history, **for the first time we care!** And caring may be the factor that ends the horror.

It all begins with talking to each other. The most important people women can talk to are their daughters. Womanhood must be reinvented, not continued like some old, wornout habit.

I had a rare and touching experience one night when I was writing the first edition of this book. For months, I had been ranting and raving at every television commercial, every movie, every antifeminist remark that escaped unwittingly from any male, including my son, and discussing the chapters of this book with my friends and family as I wrote them. Not a newspaper article, an unfair job situation that came to my attention, an action taken by a woman politically, escaped my comment. The household had had quite a dose of women's affirmative action. But since my daughter at the time was young, I had no real notion about how much of it was affecting her. That truly, in the deepest part of her, she understood, I saw during a game of charades.

She pointed upward for the first part of the word in a movie title, and as our guess was incorrect, she began on the second part of the word. She made a rocking motion with her arms, as if to rock a baby. My son and I guessed words like mother, nurse, grandmother, nanny, while my daughter grew more and more impatient and puzzled. She didn't change her motion, but went on rocking harder than ever. Several times in a row she went over the title, first pointing upward, then making the rocking-the-baby motion. Finally, we gave up, and she said, "Oh, for goodness sake, it was so easy. *The Godfather* is the answer. You were so busy thinking of mothers when I rocked the baby, that's why you didn't get it. Why couldn't you think of fathers rocking a baby?"

Why indeed! We older ones have to be trained to think what, thank heaven, came perfectly naturally to her. Feminism may not have reached every corner of my mind yet, but my daughter is part of a whole new generation who, I hope, will have no truck with stereotyped sex roles, who will not think of "men's work" and "women's work," of man as the provider and woman as the childbearer, of man as the strong, and woman as the one who needs to be taken care of. The past is male. No getting around it. The future must be, not female, but androgynous. This isn't a question of being true to your badly-trained self, but true to the truth. Not everybody is going to make it. Nature didn't expend as much effort making some people as others, and there will always be those girls fleeter of foot and purpose than others. Help them.

You will make, hopefully, different choices than your mothers. But what we are all learning, all the generations together, is that it is a wonderful thing to be a woman, a strong, independent, able women who is free to stretch and stretch and stretch until she can admire herself because of her own efforts rather than seek admiration in the eyes of a boy or a man.

Never mind the jeers of those who are quick to remind us of what we have not yet done. Who knows what women will accomplish when they have learned finally to be free? Who knows what the intelligence of women will contribute to the world now that the search of women for themselves has finally begun?

Index

A

Abandonment 201

Abortion 71, 81, 160, 161, 215
  Roe vs. Wade 71, 81

Abuse xiii, 28, 40, 74, 120, 163, 203, 216

Achievement 5, 9, 14, 15, 17, 20, 30, 41, 50, 55, 214

Activism/Activist 98, 134, 146, 188, 192, 214

Advertising/media 5, 9, 10, 31, 61, 66, 83, 182, 183, 216

Affirmative action 71, 217

African-American girls 8, 19, 34, 49, 50, 54, 64, 70, 79, 82, 120, 132, 135, 137, 141, 146, 147, 148, 172, 177, 192, 211

AIDS xiii, 21, 163, 182

Appearance 85, 90

Approval 4, 14, 17, 20, 30, 159, 204, 210, 211

Arts 19, 37, 53, 54, 55, 56, 59, 115, 124

Asian-American girls 8, 19, 34, 64, 137

Assertiveness 12, 50, 51, 169, 209

B

Babies xvii, 6, 10, 44, 48, 49, 60, 96, 116, 131, 152

Beauty game 83, 88, 91

Birth control 98, 134, 155, 215

Black women/girls 5, 8, 19, 34, 49, 50, 54, 64, 70, 79, 82, 120, 132, 135, 137, 141, 146, 147, 148, 172, 177, 192, 211

C

Career x, 9, 10, 19, 20, 24, 27, 36, 37, 40, 42, 50, 56, 58, 59, 77, 81, 95, 106, 130, 147, 152, 170, 171, 172, 177, 184, 191, 193, 195, 196, 207, 208, 209, 210, 214, 229

Child abuse 74, 216

Child care 37, 39, 49, 96, 153, 176, 207

Child rearing 36, 39, 49, 58, 75, 77, 80, 81, 93, 97, 99, 100, 106, 107, 109, 111, 115, 134, 150, 152, 154, 169, 176, 177, 184, 196, 200, 205, 206, 207, 208, 209

Children 4, 5, 6, 7, 27, 64, 71, 72, 73, 81, 151

Choices 37, 157, 199, 209, 218

Civil rights 80, 141, 147, 158, 159

College 11, 33, 35, 36, 38, 39, 40, 41, 44, 45, 66, 67, 88, 91, 105, 156, 188, 192, 206

Condoms 155

Contraception 98, 134, 215

Creativity 58, 60

Credit, women's 78, 79

D

Dating 23, 26, 158

Daughters 6, 56, 73, 99, 119, 124, 154, 202, 204, 206, 217

Day care 10, 36, 72, 81, 82, 208, 214

Dependency xii, 5, 34, 95

Depression 31, 96, 97, 99, 204, 230

Discrimination xix, 38, 40, 41, 54, 70, 78, 80, 97, 101, 160, 161, 188, 191, 216

Discussion groups 133, 179, 188

Divorce 9, 34, 44, 48, 74, 76, 136, 188, 200, 205, 216

Double standard 27, 136, 169

Dropping out 17, 173

Drugs 20, 82, 182, 189, 211, 216, 230

E

Earnings 39, 46, 49, 75, 116, 126, 184, 193, 196, 197, 206, 210

Eating disorders xvi, 31, 188, 230

Education x, 34, 36, 37, 38, 40, 41, 46, 59, 67, 72, 80, 82, 88, 101, 123, 124, 125, 126, 127, 129, 130, 141, 147, 156, 160, 171, 173, 175, 192, 193, 206, 209, 210, 215

Teachers 13, 14, 15, 19, 137, 169, 171, 174, 186, 192

Textbooks 8, 14, 174, 216

Title IX 38, 80, 171

Equal Pay Act 46, 80
Equal rights amendment 71, 80, 160, 161
Equality x, 18, 34, 45, 53, 55, 72, 73, 109, 112, 115, 140, 146, 160, 168, 193, 209
Erikson, Erik 153
Expectations xiv, 4, 6, 12, 13, 17, 93, 97

F

Fathers 6, 7, 27, 60, 72, 77, 85, 87, 91, 95, 168, 176, 185, 188, 193, 206, 210, 218
Feminine xiii, 9, 13, 19, 26, 29, 30, 37, 40, 41, 49, 94, 171, 176, 180, 182, 183, 184, 203, 210
Feminism 54, 81, 128, 130, 133, 134, 138, 140, 141, 143, 145, 147, 151, 159, 161, 163, 167, 179, 195, 218, 227, 228
Feminist 38, 54, 81, 98, 126, 128, 130, 133, 134, 138, 140, 141, 142, 145, 146, 147, 148, 151, 152, 153, 161, 163, 191, 195, 227, 228

Feminist struggle 127, 133, 140, 142, 145, 173
Freedom 99, 110, 115, 123, 128, 134, 145, 146, 158, 159, 168, 174, 186, 187, 208, 210, 214
Freud, Sigmund 13, 149, 150, 151, 152, 157, 189
Friedan, Betty 100, 157, 160, 163, 227

G

Gender bias 38, 59, 72, 101, 120, 171
Girls and boys 16, 23, 26, 179
Dating 23, 24, 25, 27, 28, 179, 180, 181
Girls in school ix, x, 10, 11, 15, 169
College 11, 33, 35, 36, 38, 39, 40, 41, 44, 45, 66, 67, 88, 91, 105, 128, 129, 141, 188, 192
Girls vs. boys 4, 5, 7, 10, 13, 15, 18, 63, 215
Grade school 17
Grades 11, 17, 35, 37, 41, 94
Grammar school 11, 12, 15

High school 11, 18, 34, 35, 44, 45, 63, 66, 141, 179, 188

Junior high school 11, 18, 179

Growing up a girl 3, 6, 21, 84, 101, 106, 168, 173

Girls vs. boys 3, 6, 7, 14

Stories 8, 14, 106, 107, 108

Toys 7, 9, 64, 168

H

Heilbrun, Carolyn 38, 99, 163

High school 11, 18, 34, 35, 40, 44, 45, 63, 66, 82, 94, 141, 179, 188, 205

Hispanic-American girls 8, 46, 55, 64

Horney, Karen 228

I

Image xiii, 83, 85, 90, 181, 214, 217

Advertising/media 5, 9, 61, 62, 63, 65, 182, 183, 216

At the mall 67, 68

Clothing 16, 29, 64, 83, 89, 145, 146, 147, 180

History 86, 117

Looks xii, xiii, 5, 16, 24, 64, 83, 88, 91

Television/movies 8, 9

Incest 74, 216

Inferiority x, 8, 13, 29, 30, 31, 99, 108, 151, 195

Intelligence ix, x, 4, 11, 14, 123, 180, 182

Interests 7, 17, 99, 105, 167

J

Jobs x, 27, 47, 49, 50, 54, 73, 77, 78, 101, 106, 134, 147, 160, 173, 188, 194, 201

Jung, Carl 151

Junior high school 11, 179

K

Krishnamurti, J. 178, 229

L

Labor force 38, 44, 48, 63

Lesbian 16, 41, 163, 178, 200, 207, 229

Liberation 53, 101, 133, 167, 179, 184, 189, 214

Lookism 5

M

Male chauvinist 53

Marriage 27, 30, 44, 50, 77, 93, 169, 199

  Divorce 9, 34, 44, 48, 74, 76, 136, 200, 205, 216

  Marriage market 7, 73, 88

  Sample marriages 201, 203, 205, 206, 209, 210

  Sex roles 75, 76, 77

  Happy housewife xvii, 41, 61, 65, 96, 157

Math skills ix, 11, 19, 20, 97, 125, 129, 169, 172

Maturity 15, 33, 44

Minority women 40, 49, 159

Money 74, 75, 77, 180, 181, 184

  Earning 46, 59, 75, 95, 196

  Expectations 25

  Sex roles and 24, 25, 28

Mothers 6, 8, 10, 25, 33, 85, 87, 91, 93, 95, 99, 158, 167, 169, 176, 181, 183, 184, 201, 203, 205, 206, 207, 216, 218

Mutilation 88

  Bound feet 43, 86, 117

  Genital 59

  Piercing 24, 87

  Self-mutilation 31

N

National Organization for Women 160, 161, 191

Native-American girls 19, 64

Networking 162, 187, 188, 197, 214, 216, 217

P

Parents 13, 17, 30, 36, 41, 45, 56, 78, 84, 98, 106, 159, 170, 171, 174, 180, 185, 186, 199, 200, 203, 206, 207, 211

  As role models 95, 98, 158

  Attitude 5, 6, 84, 170, 199

Pay, equal x, 34, 46, 80, 82, 190, 215

Personal identity 3, 31, 32, 119, 130, 153, 229

Pleasing others 5, 66, 89, 94

Popularity 5, 106, 158, 204

Pregnancy xvi, 20, 82, 134, 154, 182, 200, 215, 216

Property rights 74, 75, 119, 129, 136, 138, 215

Psychological distress xv, 31, 67, 90, 96, 97, 99, 176, 203, 204, 208, 230

Psychology
    Science of 149, 151, 152

R

Racism 21, 34, 40, 82, 159, 216

Rape xiii, xvi, 40, 71, 74, 121, 216, 230
    Date rape 40, 182

Reading skills x, 28, 59

Relationships 4, 23, 26, 27, 28, 72, 96, 99, 105, 121, 169, 209

Resources 162, 163, 191, 227

Rights 69, 70, 71, 72, 77, 79, 80, 98, 99, 111, 117, 119, 120, 123, 126, 128, 129, 130, 135, 136, 137, 138, 140, 141, 146, 156, 158, 159, 160, 161, 162, 163, 173, 183, 215, 216

S

Salaries 75, 77, 94, 193, 197, 206

Science and girls xi, 11, 13, 19, 20, 64, 125, 129, 162, 169, 170, 172, 193, 202

Self worth xii, xv, 17, 91, 96, 154, 167, 172, 192, 195, 203

Self-esteem 154, 188, 192, 229, 230

Sex 28, 182
    Abortion 71, 81, 160, 161, 215
    Birth control 98, 134, 155, 159, 215
    Diseases xiii, 20, 78, 182
    Pregnancy xiii, 20, 41, 82, 154, 182, 200, 216
    Safe sex 29
    Sexual desire 28, 29, 155

Sex object 45, 63, 89, 213, 215

Sex roles ix, xi, xii, xv, xvi, xvii, xviii, 4, 5, 6, 7, 10, 12, 13, 14, 16, 19, 25, 27, 29, 41, 45, 62, 66, 94, 97, 99, 105, 110, 134, 156, 157, 171, 174, 175, 176, 177, 183, 185, 201, 203, 218
    Changing 105, 106
    History 147, 148, 149

Sexism xviii, xix, 5, 16, 21,

27, 34, 82, 125, 159, 163, 168, 174
Sexual abuse 28, 163
Sexual harassment xiii, 28, 74, 185, 191, 216, 228, 230
Sexuality 15, 109, 178, 211
 Homosexuality 16, 41, 163, 178, 200, 207, 211, 229
Sports xi, 18, 21, 162, 172, 174, 182, 189, 229
Steinem, Gloria 137, 154, 161, 163, 188
Survival 12, 213

T

Teachers, attitudes 13, 14, 15, 19, 137, 169, 171, 174, 186, 192
Teenage pregnancy 154, 216
Textbooks 8, 14, 174, 216
Think straight 31, 32, 177, 185
 Attitude 183, 186, 189
 Awareness 174
 Image 68
 Women's rights 82
Title IX 38, 80, 171

V

Verbal skills xi, 4, 15, 169
Violence 21, 59, 87, 117, 118, 120
 Date rape 40, 182
 Gangs 29, 162, 188, 211, 230
 Rape 40, 71, 74, 121, 216, 230
Vote 69, 70, 71, 74, 119, 130, 138, 141, 142, 145, 146, 147, 148, 160, 195, 216

W

Wages 129, 136
White women 34, 50, 65, 70, 120, 123, 137, 141, 177, 211
Women 33
 And men 95, 99, 105, 106
 Artists 54, 55, 56, 57, 60
 As "children" 66, 78, 95, 110, 113, 123, 167
 As housewives 75, 93, 98, 100, 195, 196
 As mothers 36, 72, 77, 81, 97
 Evolution of 113, 114, 115, 116

Great women 120

History xix, 105, 109, 110, 117, 118, 119, 127, 133, 134, 141, 155, 158, 160

Minority 34, 40, 49, 50, 159, 172

Myths 194

Quotes about 106, 107, 108, 109, 110, 111, 124, 125, 127, 128, 129, 130, 131, 132, 135, 138, 139, 140, 153, 154

Writers 38, 50, 57, 58, 60, 86, 120, 228

Women and politics 47, 70, 71, 72, 74, 79, 81, 111, 117, 120, 123, 135, 146, 159, 192, 202

Women and religion 74, 106, 107, 108, 109, 120, 136, 139, 162, 200

Women and the arts 53, 54, 55, 56, 57, 85, 173

Women at work xi, xix, 43, 47, 48, 183, 184, 187, 196

Criticism 47, 48, 49, 50

Equal pay x, 34, 40, 44, 45, 46, 81, 101, 147, 160, 190, 214, 215

Expectations 8, 19, 20, 170

Inequality 47, 48

Women in college 33, 38, 39, 40

Discrimination 36, 37

Getting into college 35, 36

Women in society 13, 35, 69, 87, 98, 114, 145, 162, 167

Women's liberation movement xix, 133, 167, 184, 189, 213, 216

Women's organizations 161

Women's rights 69, 72, 78, 123, 130, 135

Abortion 71, 80

Changing 111

Education 130

Equal Employment Opportunity Commission 80

Equal Rights Amendment 71, 80, 160, 161

Fifteenth Amendment 69

Laws 78

Nineteenth Amendment 70, 142

U.S. Constitution 69

Voting 69, 70, 138, 142

Worldwide 71, 72, 73, 74, 81

Suggested Reading
And Selective Bibliography

In this bibliography, only books especially interesting to teenage girls are listed. Most of the works that are fundamental to contemporary feminism have been mentioned in the text: Simone deBeauvoir's *The Second Sex* (1968) about the historical status of women; Betty Friedan's *The Feminine Mystique* (1964) about the exploitation of women; Vivian Gornick's *Women in Sexist Society* (1971) which contains essays by modern feminists on the role of women; Kate Millet's *Sexual Politics* (1970) on the subjugation of women; Germaine Greer's *The Female Eunuch* (1971), about women still deformed by, in bondage to men; Elaine Morgan's *The Descent of Woman* (1972), a reinterpretation of evolution in the light of the female sex; Virginia Woolf's *A Room of One's Own* (1929), an exquisite essay by the great woman writer on the difficulties all women face in trying to achieve in the professional world. Writings by Karen Horney (psychologist), Dorothy West (Harlem Renaissance novelist and journalist), Toni Morrison (novelist), Doris Lessing, Margaret Mead, the New York City's Commission in Women's Role in Contemporary Society, Anais Nin, Shulamith Firestone, have also informed this book.

Major sources for the facts and statistics in this book were newspapers and magazines, government publications, almanacs, and books that deal with feminism, the feminist movement, and the lives and thoughts of women.

AAUW Report. *How Schools Shortchange Girls*. New York: Marlowe & Co., 1995. The American Association of University Women's shocking report about second-class treatment and educational opportunity for girls, grades K-12. Also check out *Hostile Hallways: The AAUW Survey on Sexual Harassment in America's Schools*, 1993. You can gradually become invisible and disappear, lose your boundaries, and ooze into any body you meet: or you can inform yourself.

Angelou, Maya. *I Know Why the Caged Bird Sings*. New York: Random House, 1970. Heroic, courageous story of childhood suffering by the great African-American poet.

Carlip, Hillary. *Girl Power: Young Women Speak Out!* New York: Warner Books, 1995. Powerful collection of writings by teenage girls, homegirls, schoolgirls, lesbians, jocks, teenage parents, high-risk girls, sorority sisters to gangmembers.

Heilbrun, Carolyn G. *Reinventing Womanhood*. New York: W.W. Norton & Co., 1979. Investigates issues of identity for 20th century American women, the problem with past role models, ways to construct new ones.

Krishnamurti, J. *The First and Last Freedom*. New York: Harper & Row, 1975. The self and its problems.

McCorduck, Pamela, and Ramsey, Nancy. *The Futures of Women*. New York: Warner Books, 1996. Based on what women are doing now, what does the future hold — backlash, utopia, status quo, separatism? Four possibilities.

McLoone, Margo, and Siegel, Alice. *The Information Please Girls' Almanac*. Boston, New York: Houghton Mifflin Company, 1995. Packed with facts about your body and mind, careers, dating, fashion, women's inventions, sports, books, Nobel prizes, girl talk.

Orenstein, Peggy. *SchoolGirls: Young Women, Self-Esteem, and the Confidence Gap*. New York: Doubleday, 1994. Raw details of girls' lives in junior high, this New York Times Notable Book of the Year presents girls from three different schools, all different racial, ethnic, economic backgrounds, dealing with sexual harassment, the second-class treatment of girls, gangs, eating disorders, sexuality, violence, rape, drugs, whatever today's girls encounter.

Pipher, Mary, Ph.D. *Reviving Ophelia: Saving the Selves of Adolescent Girls*. New York: Ballentine Books, 1994. The world of teenage girls, its daily dangers, its depressions, addictions, suicide attempts, anorexia, boy and school and parent problems, and how parents can help.

Steinem, Gloria. *Revolution from Within: A Book of Self-Esteem*. Boston: Little, Brown and Company, 1993. For two decades, Steinem led a social revolution against injustice to girls and women — this is about the inner revolution that needs to take place, the self-help guidance, the need for women to look inside themselves and to communicate with each other, bond together, form groups to liberate their lives.

BICK PUBLISHING HOUSE
PRESENTS

7 BASIC MANUALS FOR
WILDLIFE REHABILITATION
by Dale Carlson and Irene Ruth

Step-by-Step Guides • Illustrated • Quick Reference for Wildlife Care
For Parents, Teachers, Librarians who want to
learn and teach basic rehabilitation

I Found A Baby Bird, What Do I Do?
ISBN: 1-884158-00-5, $9.95

I Found A Baby Duck, What Do I Do?
ISBN: 1-884158-02-1, $9.95

I Found A Baby Opossum, What Do I Do?
ISBN: 1-884158-06-4, $9.95

I Found A Baby Rabbit, What Do I Do?
ISBN: 1-884158-03-x, $9.95

I Found A Baby Raccoon, What Do I Do?
ISBN: 1-884158-05-6, $9.95

I Found A Baby Squirrel, What Do I Do?
ISBN: 1-884158-01-3, $9.95

*Endorsed by
Veterinarians, Wildlife
Rehabilitation Centers,
and National Wildlife
Magazines*

First Aid For Wildlife
ISBN: 1-884158-14-5, $9.95

**Wildlife Care For Birds And Mammals
7-Volume Compendium**
ISBN: 1-884158-16-1, $59.70

AVAILABLE AT YOUR LOCAL BOOKSTORE FROM:
BOOKWORLD, BAKER & TAYLOR BOOK COMPANY,
AND INGRAM BOOK COMPANY

Authors

Photo: Monica Feldak

Dale Carlson

Author of over fifty books, adult and juvenile, fiction and nonfiction, Carlson has received three ALA Notable Book Awards, and the Christopher Award. She writes novels and psychology books for young adults, and general adult nonfiction. Among her titles are *The Mountain of Truth* (ALA Notable Book), *Where's Your Head?* (Christopher Award), *Girls Are Equal Too* (ALA Notable Book), *Wildlife Care for Birds and Mammals.* Carlson has lived and taught in the Far East: India, Indonesia, China, Japan. She teaches writing and literature during part of each year. She lives in Connecticut with orphaned cats, raccoons, squirrels, and skunks.

Photo: Photos in a Flash

Hannah Carlson, M.Ed., C.R.C.

Past Director of Developmental Disabilities at The Kennedy Center for the Mentally Disabled, at West Haven Community House, Hannah Carlson is author of *Living with Disabilities*, based on a six-volume series of Basic Manuals for Friends of the Disabled, including *I Have a Friend with Mental Illness, I Have* a *Friend with Mental Retardation, I Have a Friend in a Wheel-chair, I Have a Friend with Learning Disabilities, I Have a Friend Who Is Blind, I Have a Friend Who Is Deaf.* She is former Senior Therapist and Vocational Counselor/Evaluator at Rusk Institute of Rehabilitation Medicine at New York University Medical Center. She has lectured and taught in her field of the developmentally and traumatically disabled, and is several times published in the international journals "Brain Injury," and in the "Journal of Applied Rehabilitation Counseling." She holds a Masters of Education in Counseling Psychology and a Masters Degree in Developmental Psychology from Columbia University. She is Founder and Director of Discovery Days Day Care Center, and lives with her children Chaney and Shannon and animals of assorted sizes in Connecticut.

Illustrator

Carol Nicklaus

Known as a character illustrator, her work has been featured in *The New York Times, Publishers Weekly, Good Housekeeping,* and *Mademoiselle.* To date she has done 150 books for Random House, Golden Press, Atheneum, Dutton, Scholastic, and more. She has won awards from ALA, the Christophers, and The American Institute of Graphic Arts.